CHRISTMAS IN THE TROPICS

A CELEBRATION OF LIFE IN MICRONESIA

JOE RACE

Trafford
PUBLISHING™

Order this book online at www.trafford.com
or email orders@trafford.com

Most Trafford titles are also available at major online book retailers.

author photo by Paila Miradora
front cover painting by Rodante Guarda

Note for Librarians: A cataloguing record for this book is available from Library and Archives Canada at www.collectionscanada.ca/amicus/index-e.html

Printed in Victoria, BC, Canada.

ISBN: 978-1-4269-1521-5 (soft)
ISBN: 978-1-4269-1522-2 (hard)

Library of Congress Control Number: 2009935509

Our mission is to efficiently provide the world's finest, most comprehensive book publishing service, enabling every author to experience success. To find out how to publish your book, your way, and have it available worldwide, visit us online at www.trafford.com

Trafford rev. 10/6/2009

 www.trafford.com

North America & international
toll-free: 1 888 232 4444 (USA & Canada)
phone: 250 383 6864 ♦ fax: 812 355 4082

POTPOURRI ABOUT LOVE, ISLANDS AND CHRISTMAS

Albert Einstein: (Explaining the concept of relativity) "When you are courting a nice girl an hour seems like a second. When you sit on a red-hot cinder a second seems like an hour. That's relativity."

British Admiral Cyprian Bridge – (1855) – on the early island days – "Those who believe that the beachcomber or the copra trader of the South Seas is necessarily a scoundrel, err grievously. There is proportionately to their numbers as much honesty, sobriety and energy amongst the traders as amongst any body of businessmen. They have their black sheep, no doubt; let the community which has none throw at them the first stone…"

Burton Hellis – The best of all gifts around any Christmas tree: the presence of a happy family all wrapped up in each other."

Charles Dickens – "I will honor Christmas in my heart, and try to keep it all the year."

Don Blanding (1894-1957): (Re: Hawaii and the tropical islands) – "If you'll take my sage advice, you won't wait to go to Heaven for a life in paradise…Buy a ticket now to the islands."

Hamilton Wright Mabie – "Blessed is the season which engages the whole world in a conspiracy of love!"

Henry Wadsworth Longfellow – "I heard the bells on Christmas Day, Their old, familiar carols play, And soft and sweet, The words repeat, Of Peace on earth, good-will to men…"

John Byron – "Christians awake, salute the happy morn, whereon the Savior of the world was born."

Josephine Daskan Bacon – "Remember this December that love weighs more than gold!"

Judge Judy on being Happy: "When you're older, hopefully you've developed the smarts to know that if you wake up in the morning and you're vertical and your kids are healthy, that's 90 percent of being happy. That's it!"

Kahlil Gibran – "Love has no other desire but to fulfill itself. To melt and to be like a running brook that sings its melody to the night. To wake at dawn with a winged heart…"

Laura Ingalls Wilder – "Our hearts grow tender with childhood memories and love of kindred, and we are better throughout the year for having, in spirit, become a child again at Christmas-time."

Mark Twain – "Man is the only animal that blushes. Or needs to…"

Mother Teresa –"We ourselves feel that what we are doing is just a drop in the ocean. But the ocean would be less because of that missing drop."

Norman Vincent Peale – "Christmas waves a magic wand over the world and behold, everything is softer and more beautiful."

Roy L. Smith – "He who has not Christmas in his heart will never find it under a tree."

W. Ronald Tucker – "For centuries, men have kept an appointment with Christmas. It means fellowship, feasting, giving and receiving, a time of good cheer, home."

Thomas Jefferson – "I predict future happiness for Americans if they can prevent the government from wasting the labors of the people under the pretense of taking care of them…"

OTHER BOOKS BY JOE RACE

Movin' On
Continuin' On
Ramblin' On
Hawaiian Paniolo
Sitting on a Goldmine
Floater on the Reef
Christmas in the Tropics
The Korean Shadow - (children)
Shrimp: The Way You Like It - (cookbook)

DEDICATION

To Santa Claus and all his little elves – Cynthia, Richard, Josh, Melinda, Jeff, Heidi, James, Sylvia, Kraig, Yoshi, Nobu, Jen, Donavan, Nikkei, Kimi, Gresil, Tony, Paila, Jae, Cody, Gabriella, Marie, Katrina, Cassandra, Alana, Nikki, Makayla, Kylie, Danny, Salvacion, and George

ACKNOWLEDGEMENTS

A special *mahalo and gracias* to my supportive family and my conscripted friends who were forced to read various drafts of this holiday story, or suffer the hunger and embarrassment in **not** being invited to one of my wife Salve's famous barbeques. They read and edited well, and stored up some extra calories before the next tsunami. Special friends include Bud and Donna White, "Banjo Dan" Hocking, Urbano Duenas, Jeff Williams, Donna Liwag, Billy Organ, Rhogel Aguilar, Cassie Nelson, Patricia Friedrich, Johnny Bowe, Juanita Mendoza, Marie Miradora and my three little assistants, Paila, Katrina and George.

Also I want to thank my Yapese friends who wish to remain anonymous, staying true to form in being "one with nature," being quiet and non-imposing, and representing the true meaning of "peace and joy." They are wonderful people.

Celebrating the birth of Jesus Christ, Christmas is an important holiday for Christians all over the world, and it's a significant celebration for bringing families and loved ones together in the spirit of peace and good will to all men. St. Nicholas, aka Santa Claus, in terms of chronological history, is a recent addition to the holiday, and he too as does Jesus in his many sermons, talks about kindness, loving one another, and giving presents and food to those less fortunate than one's self.

Happiness, joy, prosperity and good health to one and all. Happy Holidays!

Come see our beautiful, tropical islands and satisfy those nagging feelings of wanderlust. Till then…

CONTENTS

PROLOGUE

There is a far-away group of is-
lands in the Pacific known as the State of Yap. You heard right, "Yep,
it's Yap." It is just a few degrees above the equator and very hot and
humid. It is the farthest west of the four states of the newly-emerged
country called the Federated States of Micronesia, and home to
about eleven thousand people. It is a very traditional locale and the
island chiefs still wield great power, even to the extent of stopping
legislation in the elected government if the matter is considered anti-
cultural in any way. The caste system was formally eliminated by
their Constitution, but is very much in place in every day activities.
There are seven tiers or ranks in the caste system, *madangadang* being of high nobility and *reisifar* (commoner) being the lowest.

The State of Yap (meaning "the land" in local parlance) consists
of three islands interconnected by bridges (Yap Island, Gail-Tomil,
and Maap), plus nearby Rumung Island and fifteen inhabited outer
islands, which stretch about 625 miles east across open ocean, with
little Satawal being the farthest east with only five hundred people.
A barrier reef surrounds the three main islands cluster, and tourists
come for the excellent diving and to view manta rays, and to watch
the dancing and listen to the Yapese distinctive music with pound-
ing, thundering drums. Four languages are spoken in Yap State –
Yapese, Ulithian, Satawalese and Wolealian – but most everybody
speaks enough English to communicate in government, business and
education.

There are sharp distinctions between *pumawn* men and *pin* women and their roles in society. Women farm and do domestic duties, while the men fish. Many women, mainly outer-islanders, still go bare-breasted, wearing only a *lava-lava*, a skirt made of hibiscus and banana fiver, or cotton cloth. It's socially proper to show bare breasts but not thighs or the legs above the knee. American men and Europeans are often called "swivel-necks," because they're just not used to seeing bare-breasted women, and when they do on Yap, it's an automatic turn-around to see if their eyes are being true. It is particularly noticeable in an air-conditioned department store.

Men and even young boys wear the *thu* (loincloth) and reflect the male's origins, an outer islander will wear white or blue, if from Yap Proper (center of government and business), the *thu* will be multi-colored and if of mixed blood, he will wear red. Betel nut chewing is universal and continual, even among the women and children. Just about everybody carries a brightly colored basket, woven from coconut leaves, that holds the necessary nut, lime and pepper leaves for the chew. Yap is jokingly called "The Land of Vampires" because the chew and saliva turn red, and spitting is a common practice all over the islands, even in community areas such athletic fields, schools, motels, just about everywhere. It is uncommon to see anyone over thirty with a full set of teeth. Mouth cancer is a problem.

The Yapese are considered the great voyagers of the Western Pacific, able to travel incredible distances in outrigger sailing canoes, using only the sun, lunar phases, stars, winds and waves, and marine and terrestrial biology as their guides. Even in the technical age of GPS, radios, cellular phones, and radar, and equipment to find fish, the Yapese still travel phenomenal distances and catch fish without the modern gadgets. Every year they win sailing contests between the other main Micronesian islands without radar and radios, and sometimes all the way to Hawaii or Saipan. They promote self-sufficiency and resource sustainability, and teach others traditional fishing practices such as *talayeru*.

As with most of the Micronesian Islands, Yap had been under the colonial control of the Spanish, German, Japanese, and the islands were deemed important because of their strategic location, and also there were copra (dried coconut), phosphates and beche-de-mer (sea cucumbers) to be harvested. After 1945 under the auspices of the United Nations and the United States, Yap was part of the political entity known as the Trust Territory of the Pacific Islands until the inhabitants established their own current government status which they negotiated in 1982. The US granted Yapese free access to the mainland for jobs, education, military enlistment, business, and travel, and also protects their borders with US military forces. Besides fishing, farming, and tourism, the main source of economic survival for the Yapese is US funds granted under the Compact of Free Association with the US, which supports most of their educational and medical services.

Community leader and teacher John Sapelalut had known only life under the Americans. He was quite satisfied with the current political configuration and had often thought of becoming a US citizen.

He had heard brutal tales about the Japanese whipping his ancestors when they didn't work hard enough and how they were forced to take Japanese classes and attempts were made by the professors to assimilate them into the Japanese culture. But the ancient caste and traditional systems of the Yapese held stronger and very few native people became "Japanese" in dress, language or thinking. As the stories were told to the young Yapese by their fathers and grandparents, the old people would laugh when they related how the Japanese became very frustrated when they wouldn't change their old ways. Sometimes the professors would get all *rau* (red) in the face with anger, and jump up and down, and threaten to have all the youngsters beaten or carried off to Japan for intensive training; but the Japanese were distracted by the war with the Americans, and towards the end of the war were only concerned about rummaging for food and basic survival. The local children were never carried off.

Christmas is a big deal on the islands – it is a major holiday with numerous celebrations. Over ninety percent of Yapese are Christians, mostly Catholic. Missionaries from the Mormons,

Baptists, Methodists, Presbyterians, and Universal churches are busily spreading the gospel according to their teachings, and also several teachers from the BaHai faith are occasionally present. It is commonly said that there are more missionaries per capita in Micronesia, than anywhere else on earth. No landmines, terrorism or ambushes to worry about. Maybe it's the great weather and pristine beaches... and the friendly people.

As always, Christmas would be important but more so this year. There would be large parties in the homes and fiestas on the beach. The John Sapelalut Family was especially looking forward to the big day and reuniting the family.

Chapter 1

REALISTIC NEWS

John Sapelalut was looking out through the window up at the high green mountains easterly on Oahu, when the physician entered his room at the Royal Hospital in Honolulu, Hawaii. John's wife, Anna, was at his side, massaging his shoulder. She was wearing a colorful Mother Hubbard island dress patterned with orchids, ginger blooms and palm trees. The room was decorated with dozens of fragrant tropical flowers.

John greeted the doctor, *"Mogethin."*

Dr. Hilario Carter was one of the most respected and recognized heart specialists in the entire Pacific Region. Being a mixture of Japanese and Caucasian, he was a handsome man, reaching just over six feet tall, extremely brilliant and academic. He looked grim and said, "John and Anna, the final tests and evaluations are in." He looked them both in the eyes, "You two have become my friends. You've been in and out of the hospital for over a year. We've made some progress in the past, but John, the news is not good."

Anna started to tear up. Her body shuddered. John asserted, "Give it to me straight, Doc. No *bula-bula*. I've been living with this condition for over five years. I can take any news, good or bad."

"John, you have deteriorated too far. You're relapsing and your body is trying to shut down. You're not a candidate for a heart transplant with complications of age and deteriorating organs. Your sixty-year-old body is tired and your veins and muscles are collapsing because of your weak heart. There might be no bouncing back this time."

"What's that mean? Give me the facts so I can enjoy my last days if that's the prognosis." Anna began sobbing and he patted her on the back, and kissed the side of her head.

"This is not only my opinion. I wanted to be sure. I ran your whole chart and X-rays by a medical committee with five cardiac specialists this morning. It is our conclusion that you've got three to four months of active life left, and then you'll most likely slip into a coma and need hospice care."

Anna asked, "What's hospice? Where do we go for that?"

"Hospice is making your last days comfortable and pain-free. You can either reserve a room in a certain part of this hospital or you can have nurses come by your Honolulu home with the medication and help keep you clean and comfortable. Turning your body over is part of the plan so you don't get nasty bedsores."

John focused again on the green mountains and then looked to the east at the magnificent Pacific Ocean. His mind was buzzing and he felt a surge of adrenaline. He asked, "Doc, do you think I have at least three months left? Can you be sure?"

Doctor Carter shrugged his shoulders and declared, "John with your positive attitude and the support by Anna, you could possibly go longer. I can't guarantee anything. Most of the time left is up to you, eating proper food, taking your medications on schedule, no alcohol or betel nut, and following the exercise program. "

John exclaimed, "I can do all that. I'm not going to die in some hospice room far away from my Micronesian islands. I'm going home to make the most of the time left. I wanna see my family, my friends and eat some fresh fish from the reef. I've got to see my sunsets and smell the fresh ocean breezes."

Anna said, "It's three months to Christmas. I know the children will be so happy to see you, and all your friends and your former students from the high school. Everyone in the village is aways asking about you. Christmas is a time of hope and joy. It'll be so special for all of us."

"It'll be a wonderful Christmas." He looked at Doctor Carter and asked, "When can I travel? I'm ready to go now."

"Give yourself a few days to build your strength. I'll get all your medications together and instructions for Anna. I also prepare a report for the doctor on the Yap Islands. Where are you going to go in the island chain?"

John laughed and said, "I'm going to a group of outer islands called Ulithi. The main islands are Asor, Falealop, Fatharai and Mogmog. Most people have never heard of Yap, let along Ulithi. We live on Falealop where the main administrative buildings are, including the high school. No doctors or hospitals there, just wide open ocean. It's a beautiful atoll with lots of palm trees and *taro* patches."

"I'll teach Anna everything that she needs to know. Nutrition is going to be all important, and you have to keep your body moving with the exercise plan. Walks on the beach will be helpful. You stop moving your body, it'll just shutdown."

"Got it. I'll follow instructions to the letter. I wanna see my family and friends and soak up some sun and feel the islands breezes on Ulithi. I wanna smell plumeria blossoms and jasmine at nighttime and I wanna see the stars so close that we can pick them like flowers." He paused and said, "Doc, you would love it there. Maybe you can come for a visit? Got a shady hammock for you, one in the morning shade and another in the afternoon as we move around the sun, so you can stay in the shade all day."

"I'll talk it over with my wife. My two teenage daughters love to snorkel."

"Doc, we can get them certified for scuba diving right away. They'll love the water, about 85 degrees with loads of fish, clams and other sea life."

Doctor Carter smiled and answered, "It could work. We've looking for an adventure vacation, something different than visiting an amusement park or a dusty old museum. My oldest daughter is an aspiring photographer. Yap would be a memorable experience, maybe give her some ideas for a career. How's the fishing for us landlubbers?"

"Lots of reef fish like tataga, hangne, rock cod and parrotfish, and plenty of open-ocean fish, big ones like yellow-fin tuna, albacore, wahoo, and fighting barracuda."

Anna said, "And I'll teach the girls about our culture, dancing the hula and local dances, singing and doing handicrafts." Enthusiasm is contagious and all three became excited about his family's possible trip to the islands.

Although his job was meaningful, Doctor Carter often found himself thinking of running away to a tropical paradise. It was an ebullient proposition. He asserted, "This could happen at Christmas time…but no betel nut. You told me how terrible that chew is and how habit-forming. I want the girls to keep all their teeth and good health."

John guffawed and said, "It's a deal, Doc. We don't chew and still have all our teeth. You know the word travel comes from the French word *travailler* which translates to toiling and laboring, like something is rigorous and tough. It's been used since about 1375 when travel was unpleasant. But that's not the case at all in our islands. You can relax and be refreshed and get all the exercise and sunshine that you can handle. You can find your own version of Shangri La. It just happens to be at the equator and not high in the mountains of Tibet."

Anna nodded in agreement.

"Now, I think I'll have a rest. Anna will call the Medical Referral Office for getting us out of here in a few days." He paused and added, "Thank you, Doc. You just added more days to my life. I'm so happy about going home. It will be good to see all my fishing amigos and all of the extended family."

Anna moved over and hugged the doctor, and whispered, "Thank you so much. In Yap, we say *kammagar*. We are so appreciative."

"Thank you also for your invitation to see your islands. I'll be checking in a few times every day to see John and making sure he's ready to travel. Yap is thousands of miles away and many hours in an airplane. It will be a strenuous journey."

Anna grimaced, "Don't we know…a very long trip."

Chapter 2

HOSPICE – ISLAND STYLE

Once John decided he wanted
to return to Yap to live out his last days, Doctor Carter and Anna
moved quickly and efficiently through the red tape of taking care
of the physician and hospital bills, rounding up the medications and
equipment, and getting the airline tickets for John's trouble-free return to Ulithi. John expressed his gratitude over and over, actually to
anyone that would listen, that he was homeward bound and would
not die in a hospice environment. His skin, lately ashen and pallid,
was taking on a healthier glow. He was still weak.

He was so glad that he wouldn't be returning to his islands in a
wooden box stored in flight cargo. He was ecstatic about walking
upright without an identifying toe tag. He had seen several corpses
rolled by him on a gurney in the hospital with the ID tag sticking
out from the covering blanket. It made him shiver just thinking of
being stored in an icebox until the loved ones came and picked him
up.

Anna had them booked from Hawaii on Continental Airlines,
with a short layover on Guam, and then to Yap. Modern times had
come to Yap, and she was able to talk to her youngest daughter Erica,
known as "Baby Girl" in the family, via satellite phone and later with
confirmation of time and itinerary through email. Erica had arranged for her father John to have a short check-up at the Yap hospi-

tal and reserved a friend's boat to take them to the Sapelalut home on Ulithi the following day

On the airline, John slept most of the way to Guam. The nine-hour flight was a smooth and routine. Every time he awoke, Anna noticed that he was grinning and looking healthier. He was thinking of his thatched hut on Ulithi and the green rolling hills of Yap. The island weather was close to perfect, always about eighty degrees, day and night, 24/7. John was already feeling that his long pants and aloha shirt were uncomfortable. He was ready to strip down and put on his *thu*.

The layover on Guam was only two hours, but he thought intensely of his son and grandson, both fighting with the Army in Iraq, when he saw the wall photos at the airport of the twenty islanders killed while serving in the Middle East. He broke from his deep thoughts when their flight was called and they soon found themselves jetting off to Yap. John was extremely happy and excited about being homeward bound, but he began struggling for air in his physical anxiety. Anna massaged his neck and shoulders and he finally calmed down and fell into a deep sleep. As they neared the Yap Airport, Anna could sense that he was dreaming about home, and was mumbling something about the lush mangrove forests along the shoreline. He awoke, bragging about "the biggest crab" that the villagers had ever seen.

Anna patted him on the arm, "So you still dreaming about the record crab that you caught when you were eleven years old."

John answered, "That's so. No one has ever come close to that size. My uncle has a photo to prove it. It was over fourteen inches from claw to tail. That crab fed five of us."

In a slow, thoughtful manner, Anna asked, "Would you wanna be eleven again?"

"Only if I could get a guarantee that I would meet you again in college."

"You're such a nice man. If you didn't see me at college, I would come looking for you. Hawaii's not that big. I would find you."

Holding her hand, he said, "Thank goodness. I can't imagine a life without you." He paused and looked out the window, "There's the airport! We're almost home."

The greetings at the Yap Airport were jubilant celebrations of residents and visitors coming and going. The people leaving for college or business, or on vacation to see their loved ones on the mainland were adorned with flowers and necklaces, and the arriving locals and tourists were welcomed with music, handshakes (even bare-knuckled rapper style), and *mwars mwars and leis* of bright island flowers. It was a scene repeated about four times a week when the "big white bird" made its stop from Guam. It had recently rained and there were a series of broken rainbows and the jungle glistened with a misty, post-drizzle shimmer.

Daughter Erica and her friends had arranged for a car to take John to the hospital for a check-up before he went to his remote island where there were no medical facilities. The local American-trained doctor took one look at John and said, "He needs an overnight stay while he catches up on his rest, and I have a chance to review his chart and to make sure his medications are adequate. The Medical Response Team doesn't get to Ulithi often enough so I want to make sure John is set up properly."

John smiled and said, "No argument from me. I need to stretch out and relax a bit. I do want to get to Ulithi tomorrow."

The local doctor replied, "We'll get you there." Anna got John settled in and after he fell asleep, she and Erica left to visit some friends and to do some shopping for their remote island.

Erica later asked, "What do you think Mom? Is Papa going to be okay way out on his home island?"

"He knows the problems with being so far away from a hospital, but it's his choice and we have to honor his wishes. He really enjoys Christmas and wants our family together. I think being home will add weeks and maybe even months to his life. He's so excited about seeing everyone, all his old friends and students, and all his extended family. It should be refreshing and inspirational for him. You know he's always been the shepherd of the family, always looking forward to bringing the whole family together."

Family members, friends and many of his old cronies visited John in the hospital that evening. Rather than bringing him canned meat and pork *chicharrones* and greasy stir-fry, he was loaded down with chicken soup, whole wheat bread and veggies, and plenty of pineapples and papaya for dessert. He kinda frowned at his tray but remembered what the doctor had said about eating properly and extending his life.

He said, "I've got an idea. I know it's crazy and expensive, and hard to do, but I want my whole nuclear family home for Christmas. I mean bring everybody back to Ulithi for a special Christmas, even our son and grandson serving in the Army in Iraq. Maybe we can get them humanitarian leave, based on my heart condition. Besides it's their second tour fighting the insurgents. I'm always afraid they're going drive over a hidden IED."

Anna smiled, "What a great idea. We can all pitch in. I still have a small bank account…and the boys in the army will have some savings."

Erica frowned. She didn't like to think about her brother and nephew being blown up. "It would be so good to see everybody again. I haven't even seen some of my other nieces and nephews. I've also got a savings account from selling my crafts and my friend's carvings to the tourists."

John concluded, "It can work. Everybody start planning and making calls. Let's plan on everyone getting here a few days before Christmas, and then they can stay over until New Year's Day." His face was flushed and his eyes were at half-mast. The medication was doing its job. It had been a long day.

Anna said, "My Sweet John, get some rest. We'll see you in the morning after you've had a good sleep. We'll try for Ulithi right after breakfast. The weather is ready to cooperate and looks perfect." She kissed him on the forehead and he slipped off into slumberland.

"Mom, let's go to the internet café and get things rolling." Erica took her mother by the arm, and as they walked past the nurse's station, she dropped off the untouched, leftover food for the workers. There were no cafeteria, laundry or janitorial services at the Yap Hospital. Other than the medical services, everything else was provided by the families of the patients. If the patient needed sheets and towels, the family would have to bring them down, and probably make the bed.

Anna and Daughter Erica pulled out their address books and started making their family contacts. Surprisingly, the telephone call went right through to the oldest son, Constantine, in Iraq in his battalion's recreation room, just outside of Baghdad.

"Mom, is that you? Where are you calling from? You sound like you're right next door."

"Hi Constantine. We're home in Yap. The satellite must be in the right place. I hope you and Andre are doing fine."

"Yep, we're okay. I just finished a patrol. He's out right now. We had a report of some spontaneous shooting and his unit is checking it out. It's a common call-out, so don't worry." He asked, "Why are you calling? What's the occasion? Andre and I don't have birthdays for another few months."

"I'm afraid it's not good news. Your father is having those damn heart problems again. I'll tell you straight. The doctor says that he only has three to six months to live. Father wants you and André home for Christmas."

"Damn, I've been worried about his health. I'll have to talk to my commander. We still have another five months to serve on this tour, but I really want to get back and see Papa."

"See what you can do. I can scan all father's medical reports, get a letter from his heart specialist, and email them to you. I can send a personal letter and ask that you and Andre be released home early for humanitarian reasons."

"Thanks, Mom. Are you on the line, Erica?"

"I'm here. We really want to see you for the holidays and we can celebrate your birthdays at the same time. We're trying to get everyone together to see Papa."

"Good. I love you guys. Hopefully will see you soon. Send the reports right away so I can start the paperwork from our end. It will be grand to see Papa, and be on our beautiful islands again. Tell him to eat only veggies and fruits, and for a special treat, maybe some almonds and walnuts. This place is a real pain - nothing but desert and blowing sand and a lot of people that wanna see us dead."

Anna reluctantly inquired, "Are you going to re-enlist?"

"Don't know for sure. Will have a long and hard talk with my gorgeous wife Belle. Oh, the latest news in the romance department; Andre has fallen in love with a soldier stationed in Germany. She's a cutie – you'll like her. They're both kinda of thinking about leaving the service and getting a college education."

Anna said, "I hope I like the girl. I sure want Andre home safe and sound, and in one piece."

He asked, "How about me, Mom?"

"Of course, you're my *numero uno* baby!"

Chapter 3

THE EARLY DAYS

Surrounded by barking dogs and chirping birds, John woke up early the next morning. The nurse had opened up his hospital window and a warm, gentle breeze was rustling the pages of his chart at the foot of his bed. He watched the flowers on his nightstand swaying back and forth, all the bright colors intermingling and making a gorgeous, natural display. It was the first time in a year that he felt so euphoric and at peace with the world. He smiled to himself and thought, "Maybe it's all the new drugs, or the right combo, or just maybe, he was home where he should be. No more prodding doctors and nurses with a million annoying questions."

He let his mind roam free without any direction and he soon found himself thinking about his early teenager days, especially about his good friend Caesar, who had drowned when he got caught in his father's fishing nets while free-diving. The current had changed mysteriously and drastically, and Caesar's father hadn't seen the boy get trapped. John had gone on many trips with the family, but on that fateful day, he had to stay home and prepare some dried copra for the ship that was coming the following week. He often wondered if he had been along on the trip, if he could have dove in and cut his friend free from the nets. He always carried a long commando-like knife.

Some days he became depressed and feeling guilty about not saving Caesar, but he always managed to escape from the funk by remembering his friend and his carefree attitude. He could almost imagine him saying, "Don't worry, John. Some days are routine, and other days are just Bad, with a capital "B". We just go along with whatever happens." He chuckled to himself, remembering the day they found a crashed World War II bomber and stripped off the wing fuel tank and fashioned it into an aluminum fishing canoe. They were the talk of the island, especially when they brought back two long stringers loaded with fish.

As good luck would have it, on one of his depression days, he walked down to the harbor and was sitting on Caesar's family canoe, reminiscing about the good times that they had shared; when a new girl to the island, maybe about fifteen, came strolling by, throwing rocks into the bay. She nodded a greeting at John and he nodded back. She kept walking and John noticed how beautiful and perfect she was. She was topless with well-developed breasts and her swaying, graceful hips were covered with a blue and green lava-lava.

When the girl reached the end of the bay, she looked back to see if John was watching. He was. She turned around and came back along the shoreline. John revved up his courage and introduced himself as she reached the canoe. John said, "Hi, I'm John. This is my island. Where's your island?"

The girl answered, "Hello, my name is Anna and my family just moved here from Woleai – it's in the center of the eastern outer islands. I'm really excited about going to high school next month. I've never been in a classroom. My mother taught me to read and write. I might have trouble with math."

"Don't worry. If you have any trouble, I can help you. I have a good report card."

"Thank you. I hope to see you again. We live in the lime-green house on the northend. Maybe you can come by and meet my parents. My father has already started a huge taro patch and is working on a scheme to bring coconuts here from the outer islands and then on to Yap for shipment to the States. He's a member of the Coconut Authority for all of Yap."

"You sound very proud of your father. How about your mother?"

"She is a beautiful woman with a big heart. She helps everyone when they're sick. She knows a lot about natural healing and some about sorcerery, but she doesn't abuse or misuse her powers. How about your parents?"

"My father also works with coconuts and copra, and sometimes *beche-de-mer* (sea slugs for food and aphrodisiacs). Our fathers probably know each other. My mother weaves baskets and coordinates the wood carvers on our island. She sells her work in Yap Proper or at the airport. Some of her most impressive baskets are requested by museums and art galleries in America and Europe. She is very talented." He hesitated and then said, "I would like to come meet your parents. Can you ask them for me?"

As Anna left, she said, "I will ask them if you can visit. I'll send you a note. Don't smoke or chew betel nut, okay? My parents disapprove because they call them "filthy habits," and they're worried about broken teeth, and mouth and lung cancer."

He waved goodbye and said, "Fine with me. I don't chew or smoke. I'll wait for your note."

She noticed that his teeth were perfect and the enamel hadn't been worn away to black stubs from chewing the nasty nut.

Two days went by and then two more days. John was getting worried that her parents would disapprove of him visiting their home. On the fifth day, a small boy arrived on a bicycle carrying a note, and said, "I'm Anna's brother. She said to give you this."

John was elated when he read the letter. Their fathers did know each other through the coconut harvesting, and Anna's father approved his visit to their *tagil* (place) on Sunday after church. Her father said that he could walk home with them after the services, and then have lunch. The note also said to bring a swimming suit because there was a nice beach in front of their home. John showed the note to his mother who said, "I know both Anna's parents. They're nice people, so I expect you to be on your best behavior…and remember to take a small gift for the mother. Mothers like to receive gifts, you know."

John couldn't ever remember being antsy and nervous about going to church. When Sunday came, he went early to the sparkling white church building and waited out front for Anna. He hid off to the side while Anna and her family went into church. He noticed that she kept looking around, hopefully for him. He sat in the back pews. Anna turned around several times, and when she saw him, she released a giant smile and raised her eyebrows, acknowledging him island-style. Her mother noticed her fidgeting in her seat and nudged her in the side. Anna gave him another secret smile and then turned to the front to listen to the sermon. The priest talked about morality and being honest and truthful with your loved ones.

After the last hymn, John waited outside for Anna and her family. His father came up behind him and said, "Let's go greet Anna's family. We already know her parents but it will nice that we introduce you, and you can introduce Anna to us. I'm sure you will be seeing a lot of each other at school and island activities."

The introductions went smoothly and when she shook hands with Anna, he noticed that her hands were small and very soft. She was wearing a bright yellow sundress and she had a matching bow in her long black hair. John thought to himself that he had never seen anyone so attractive. She was more beautiful than the tropical flowers or a golden sunset. Both of her parents were friendly and invited John's parents to their home for lunch. The father said that he had caught a thirty-pound tuna that he was ready to put on the barbeque. The father took John by the arm and said, "*Ub* (come)! You can help with the barbeque fire." John gave the mother a bag of fresh cucumbers and tomatoes from the family garden.

John's parents said that they had to go to Yap Proper to see some friends and to handle some business arrangements. They said that they would all get together next weekend at their home.

After lunch, Anna showed John some of her books and her shell collection. She had a dozen books about the ocean, especially the reefs, and showed him her favorite shells like the rare coral hatchet, and many common shells, but excellent specimens such as a cowrie, mussel, barnacle, butter clam, conch, and a spectacular nautilus. He was impressed with her enthusiasm, and was especially happy when she said that she wanted to go swimming. He enjoyed being with her alone. Her parents decided to rest in the shade and told the young-sters they would watch from their cabana. John went to the rear of the house and changed into his swimming shorts. When he came out onto the beach, Anna was running for the water, topless, wearing only her lava-lava. Again, John was over-whelmed with her beauty and her femininity, and her gorgeous body. He was careful not to look at her too closely, and embarrass himself physically with too much carnal interest.

Their pleasant Sunday afternoons continued, even after school started. Though home-schooled, Anna excelled in her studies and only had a few struggles with her pre-algebra. John helped her over the rough spots, and afterwards sitting on the beach, they would talk about their futures and where they wanted to go in the world. They had a few stolen kisses but nothing more. They were both clear about avoiding pregnancy and bringing their plans to quick stop and end-ing up locked into a limited life on the remote islands. They wanted more. John planned to be a teacher, and Anna a trained, skilled artist. They were interested in colleges in Oregon and looked for financial aid sources. But more than that, they wanted to be close to each other and in their senior year of high school started to discuss marriage.

John said that college and marriage could work, since both of them had goals and dreams, and did not drink or go to frequent parties. Anna often said, "We'll be the most boring college students ever, al-ways studying and planning for our future careers."

John replied, syrupy but well-received, "What else do we need? We have each other."

"I know you. You'll also need cinnamon rolls, ice cream and pea-nut-butter cookies."

"Gotta have food for survival and nourishment."

John spoke to his parents and won approval for the marriage after he and Anna graduated from high school and were both eighteen.

John's parents invited Anna and her folks over for a feast to discuss the marriage. The youngsters knew that the fathers had already spoken and that Anna's father had approved. The feast was the village's way of showing to everyone that marriage was a serious matter, that the parents were involved in the decision, and to set a date for the actual marriage.

The feast went well, lots of taro, *koko* (pickled cucumber), ribs and fish with finadene (soy juice, lemon, peppers, and onions sauce), red rice, and plate after plate of pineapple, papaya, mangos, star apples, bananas and differently prepared coconut dishes. The fathers spoke and gave their support, and now the couple was officially engaged. The priest gave his blessing. Anna and the mothers, and the aunties and female cousins, went to work and planned the most beautiful and meaningful wedding that the couple could ever imagine. The college loans and scholarships came through, and they would start college a month after the wedding. They laughingly called their upcoming college days as "the longest honeymoon that anyone had ever planned."

On the day of the wedding, hundreds of people came from all the Yap Islands, including the northern and western outer islands. It was indeed a glorious celebration including dancing on the *wunbey* and music, and community singing. There was even a man that played the old traditional nose flute and the dancers did the ancient *laiuka* stick dance. As John thought back, he could hear all the wonderful voices and greetings, and see all the familiar faces, many of whom had passed on. He also clearly remembered their first night together at a hotel in the main town on Yap called Colonia. They were both virgins and initially there was a little bit of fumbling, but soon they fell into each other smoothly and with love and deep feelings. Anna was on birth control, neither of them wanting children right away.

Anna said, "I think you've done this before. You seem skilled."

John answered, "No, no ever, but I read a lot of books and watched those bold movies."

"I'm glad. Maybe we can watch movies together. I was scared at first being alone with you and no chaperone, but no more. You are very nice. I love you, *Garfoko* (beloved one)."

CHRISTMAS IN THE TROPICS

"Me, too." He hesitated and then whispered, "That was lame. I love you too, and forever. You are so beautiful."

Cupid shot his little arrows deep into their hearts. As they later learned in their chemistry and psychology classes, their brains were under the influence of dopamine and nonepinephrines, commonly known as infatuation and romantic love. Falling in love led to craving, obsessive thoughts, focused attention and wanting to become part of the other person. These reactions are hard wired not to last, and the most wonderful, soaring feelings known to mankind amounts to no more than a narcotic high, a temporal stage of mania. But they learned that human bodies can't be in that state all the time, or the body would fizzle and die.

These love chemicals are measured by scientists in a trillionth of a gram which is a pictogram. The young lovers also viewed MRI scans and they saw that the brains of new lovers light up and are dramatically active. There are two shrimp-size things on either side of the brain called the caudate nuclei. These are the glands that operate bodily movement and the body reward systems, like the mind's network for general arousal, sensations of pleasure, and the motivation to gain rewards. When lovers look at each other, these changes are sent to the tiny ventral tegmental area, a little pod-size area that's send the dopamine into spinning energy. The MRI also showed that serotonin, another neurotransmitter in the brain associated with obsession, depression and racing thoughts, was greatly affected by romance and the surging dopamine.

John recalled that when the brain is officially in love, it starts driving the lover crazy with possession and lust, like you must be with the other person all the time. Oxytocin and other chemicals kick in, surging through the brain to make the lovers bond with other, producing a lower, more sustainable relationship. Sometimes drama develops when the excitement slows down, and people then start looking at more highs with big risks, addiction, additional lovers, physical pain and obsessive disorders. Sustainable new-lover passion has to end and is often misguided by expectations that are placed beyond reason and good sense. Sometimes in songs and stories continuing and glorifying never-ending love too much is a disservice to young couples. Shakespeare told his listeners, "Passion is true love's fool's gold, a flamboyant dead end on the evolutionary chain of primate happiness…"

John remembered all the exciting times with Anna and how their relationship, after a few lows and many highs, moved into the long-lasting, mature stage of longevity. He didn't care about scientific explanations, he just knew he still loved her with all his heart and soul. He knew that he came into life naked and alone, and knew that he would leave the same way, but to him, it was unimaginable without his Anna. Almost like a little kid, he muttered, "It just isn't fair. I must have her with me all the time."

John was startled and broken from his reverie when the hospital nurse said, "Let's get you ready for your trip. The doctor said that you're able to travel. I'll get all your medications and directions ready, but first, let's get your breakfast."

The nurse gave him a tray with plates of fruits, taro, coconut and vegetables, no meat, except for a slice of tuna. John asked, "Is this all? No rice?"

"That's it. We want to keep you living trim and healthy, and don't be eating all that greasy food out on your island."

John said, "You're right, but I'd sure like some bacon and eggs, and some fried rice."

"Ain't going to happen here, Oh Great Teacher! Eat up. Your family will be here soon."

An hour later, Anna showed up with her friend, the local beautician and good friend, Ruby. Before John could utter any resistance about all the attention, they had him sitting in a chair and went to work on his hair and nails. By the time the rest of the family showed, including the boat operator, John was groomed to near perfection. Erica brought him a new aloha shirt with a pattern of canoes, coconut trees and plumerias, and a new pair of blue surfer shorts. They knew that he would look good in town and maybe on the boat, but once he was his home island, he would jump into his thu and wear nothing else unless he had to come to town for business or medical reasons. They had to insist that he not start chewing betel nut again.

CHRISTMAS IN THE TROPICS

Erica also brought him an ornate walking stick made out of man-grove wood. It had been designed and finished in oils by one of Anna's artist friends. He thanked her for the special thought, and said, "Now I've got something to chase off those feral dogs." He paused and said, "And also some of your bad boyfriends."

"Father, you know I don't have a boyfriend."

"Well, just in case of the guys show up from your school days." In fun, she gently slapped him on the shoulder.

John headed for the boat, followed by dozens of his friends and former students. He felt strong, smiled and waved as he made the short walk to the harbor.

In the crowd, a twelve-year-old boy said to his older companion, "Who is that guy? What all the hoopla and yelling about?"

"That's John Sapelalut. He was voted the best teacher in Yap five different times. He also wrote instruction books for teachers."

"Yeah, I've heard of him. He must be very famous. He looks very distinguished and important. He's like a *pilune* (chief)."

Chapter 4

JOHN, THE A-1 TEACHER

John was one of the most respected teachers in all of Micronesia. There were many reasons for this; he was educated, brilliant, caring, and knowledgeable but more than that, he was passionate about his subjects. He tried to relate everything to his beloved ocean and homeland, and was always concerned about the islands and the ocean, and preserving the earth for the future generations.

When you took his classes, the student got the basics of reading, writing and arithmetic, but he always involved the oceans and the planet in some way. He would let you know that Micronesia's land area covers about 1,245 square miles and the ocean area about 4,5000,000 square miles, but also he would let the students know that the total square miles for the Pacific is 173,700,000 square miles, about one-third of the earth's surface. Then he would do some addition and subtraction problems, and then convert the square miles into square kilometers and vice-versa. He liked to stump the students with the question about the deepest point in any ocean in the world, and then the students would find out that the deepest point was right in their backyard, the Mariana Trench 11.034 miles deep.

Countless unspoiled places exist on the thousands of islands, 125 of which are regularly populated. Micronesia, meaning small islands, contains four great archipelagos: the Marshalls, Gilberts, Carolines and Mariana, mostly all north of the equator. The largest volcanic island is Guam (209 square miles) Babeldaob in the Republic of Palau (153 square miles) and Pohnpei, the Garden Isle (129 square miles). In lagoon area, Kwajalein, the US Missile Base, is the world's largest atoll (839 square miles, while inland area faraway Christmas (150 square miles) is the biggest coral atoll island.

There is great geologic variation in Micronesia's islands. Some are high (and cool) with volcanic peaks, others low islands of sand and coral. All of the Marshalls and Gilberts are coral atolls or islands. John would teach about how Global Warming was possibly going to impact the populations of these low-lying islands. Although still controversial in theory, some scientists have predicted that the water levels will rise by three feet in fifty years, ten feet by the year 2100. If it happens, on atolls this will mean the intrusion of more salt water into the groundwater supply, especially if accompanied by droughts. If the sea level rises more quickly than the coral reef can grow upward, lagoons could lose their vitality and islands would become more exposed to storms. In time, entire populations could be forced to evacuate and whole countries like the Marshalls or Kiribati could be flooded. This surprising variety of situations and landforms makes Micronesia a geologist's and researcher's dream. For example, Yap is an uplifted section of the Asian continental shelf, which floated away. John would ask the audience for their opinions, which is the case in which many of these changes will develop.

Sometimes Anna sat in on his lectures and was often amazed how John could talk about Micronesia with all its details and history without looking at his notes. She knew teaching and the environment were his passions.

There were always questions about the volcanic islands. High or low, all the islands have a volcanic origin best explained by what the scientists call the Conveyor Belt Theory. A crack or "hot spot' opens in the sea floor and volcanic material escapes upward. A submarine volcano builds up slowly until the lava finally breaks the surface, forming a volcanic island. The Pacific Plate moves northwest about four inches a year; thus, over geologic eons a volcano disconnects from the hot spot or crack from which it emerged. As the old volcanoes move on, new ones appear to the southeast and the older islands are carried away from the cleft in the earth's crust which they were born.

He explained that the island then begins to sink under its own weight, perhaps only a half-inch a century, and erosion cuts into the volcano by this time extinct. In the warm, clear waters a living coral reef begins to grow along the shore. As the island subsides, the reef continues to grow upward. In this way, a lagoon forms between the reef and the shorelines of the slowly sinking island. The reef marks the old margin of the original island.

The whole process is helped along by rising and falling ocean levels during ice ages. Rainwater causes a chemical reaction, which converts the porous limestone into compacted dolomite, giving the reef a denser base. Eventually, as the volcanic portion of the island sinks completely into the lagoon, the atoll reef is the volcanic island's only remnant.

At the hot spot moves southeast, in an opposite direction to the sliding Pacific Plate (and shifting magnetic pole of the earth), the process is repeated time and again, until whole chains of islands ride the blue Pacific Ocean. In the Marshalls, Gilbert and Line Islands this northwest-southeast orientation is clearly visible. Although the Carolines are more scattered, the tendency from Namonuito to Kapingamarangi or Kosrae, is still discernible. In every case, the islands, at the southeast end of the chains are the youngest. It is a general rule throughout the Pacific including the South Seas.

The students would bring this information home and then their parents would ask for public presentation. They and their ancestors had lived on the islands for centuries but they never knew how they were created except through local legends and folklore. The life of an atoll was always one of John's favorite lectures.

He would start with a definition. A circular or horse-shaped coral reef bearing a necklace of sandy slender islets of debris thrown up by storms, surf, and wind is known as an atoll. The central lagoon of huge Kwajalein atoll is more than eighty miles wide; but the width of dry land on an atoll is usually less than a mile from inner to outer

CHRISTMAS IN THE TROPICS

beach. Entire land-locked lagoons are rare – passages through the barrier reef are usually found on the leeward side. Atolls are seldom higher than fifteen feet. Because of this low elevation the best way to view the concept is up in an airplane.

A raised or elevated atoll is one that has been pushed up by some trauma of nature to become a coral platform rising as much a 200 feet above sea level. Steep, cave-pocked oceanside cliffs frequently surround raised atolls. A good example of this type is eight square mile Nauru. John would then show slides of the various types of atolls.

On a local level, two current practices are also harming atolls and their lagoons. First, there is increasing evidence that atoll islands form and then other reform as the ocean takes sand from one place to another. Traditional societies could move with the islands' shifts. Of course, with modern notions of property and boundaries, islanders are more likely to build sea walls and similar structures to stop these processes. But these processes might be necessary for the health of the atoll.

Additionally, particularly on populous atolls outlaying islanders often wish to be connected to the most populous island, which may have electricity, government services and jobs. Since the atoll countries are not wealthy, such islands usually are connected by causeways, rather than by high suspension bridges. These causeways, usually built with an insufficient number of costly culverts, interfere with ocean tides that had previously flushed the lagoon to keep it clean and free of bacteria. Along with these issues, as John would point out, was the growing amount of garbage that ended up either in the lagoon or in the water table that was not biodegradable, such aluminum, diapers, car batteries, and other discards that wouldn't dissolve.

John organized a committee that wrote the rules of the reef, not only for tourists but also for locals, while diving or exploring. They simply said:

- *Resist wearing gloves so that you avoid the temptation to touch.*
- *Do not collect live or even dead coral or shells.*
- *Establish natural buoyancy and keep fins off the bottom.*

- *Avoid damage to reef life through carelessly moving equipment*
- *Never chase, ride or harass aquatic life.*
- *Do not spear or collect fish while using scuba.*
- *Do not throw anything out of the boat, not cigarettes or plastic containers.*

John's classes also included numerous field trips and learning took place in the water or at the seashore, and not in some stuffy, hot classroom. Many of his students became inspired and developed his passion for nature, and went on to college to major in oceanography, biology and other sciences.

One of his assignments was for the junior high students to define the various corals of the Pacific, such as acropora, staghorn fire, mushroom, elkhorn, honeycomb and brain. Then they would be off to the reef, and afterwards would be to draw and color the corals. He would follow this up with the life on the reef studies, such as the many, multi-colored fish, the crown-of-thorns starfish, sea ananeme, sharks, eels, trumpet fish and along the shore, the coconut crab, monitor lizard, geckos and skinks, and turtles sunning themselves. By the time the student got to high school, he expected the students to be scuba certified and able to use underwater camera for their reports in full living color.

Each senior class would develop rules for their ocean ventures. He told the class to think of the ocean as a friend or a lover, but one known to have a temper at times. The senior class developed these rules for their time in the ocean, to stay relatively safe:

- *Remember we are land mammals and the ocean is not our natural habitat.*
- *Know your limits – don't exceed them.*
- *Seek out advice from locals – they know their part of the ocean.*
- *Realize that ocean creatures view you as an unwelcome intruder.*
- *In time of trouble, use your brain before your muscles.*
- *Never, ever think you have the ocean all figured out.*
- *Always have a buddy.*

CHRISTMAS IN THE TROPICS

Besides being a great, very professional teacher, he was a devoted, church-going family man. His reputation was sterling and he continued to be highly respected throughout his career and as one of the clan leaders on Ulithi.

His village was waiting for their hero, and being home for the Christmas holidays was extra special.

Chapter 5

CONSTANTINE AND ANDRE

First Sergeant Constantine Sapelalut was assigned to Camp Freedom in the Green Zone of Baghdad. He was a top-notch soldier, trained and skilled in the leadership of troops. He knew his soldiers came first and he kept them safe and prepared as much as possible, and carefully plotted out every course of action. In his first tour of Iraq, he had lost two men to IED's (Improvised Explosive Devices), in a humvee that had not been properly armored. Since then, the Army had demanded more armament, and the new bottom and side plating saved dozens of lives. Unfortunately, many of the explosions caused terrible, ugly injuries such as massive burns, head and neck injuries, and lost of limbs. Constantine admired the injured soldier's determination to live but often wondered himself if he would want to be an invalid the rest of his life and have to cared for, just to eat or go to the bathroom. He thought about mental stability after such horrendous wounds.

Constantine found himself growing increasingly angry at the Iraqi people in general for letting the insurgents ruin their lives. It wasn't safe for the locals to go to the market for food, and the cowardly enemy often sat high in an apartment house, watching television and eating snacks, and then set off the devices down on the road with their cell phones when the American soldiers were moving to help other Iraqis. Oftentimes, more local people were killed than the soldiers. The senseless mutilation puzzled him every day and he was trying to be careful that his impressions of any success were offset by the insurgent's vicious maiming and killing.

It was sad to get the phone call from his mother, Anna, about his father's deteriorating condition. Because of his military record, he was certain that he and his son Andre could get the time off. He called the Communications Section and asked them to watch for any information coming from his mother, or his father's doctor. The communications soldier on duty said that the email would be up and running in about two hours. He called the commander's aide-de-camp, explained the situation, and made an appointment with the commander for the following afternoon.

Just after he finished his phone call, a fellow sergeant came running in, and excitedly said that the Second Platoon was locked down under heavy fire about fifteen miles from the camp. They had been ambushed with rockets and rifle fire. Constantine knew his son was out on patrol and that he was assigned to that unit.

He asked, "Are they calling for back-up? Do they help from other platoons?"

"Right now, they'll calling for helicopter support. Need a coupla of missiles to take out some concrete buildings where the enemy is hiding."

"Anyone hit on our side?"

"They've also asked for a medivac once the enemy is neutralized."

"What else?"

"There's also a Marine sniper unit on a rooftop about three buildings away. The choppers know they're there so there won't a friendly-fire screw-up. According to the platoon's radioman, the snipers haven't been identified yet, and they've already taken out three insurgents."

"That's good news. When the choppers arrive, the enemy will likely get in high gear and vamoose." Constantine knew his son was in the middle of the mess and would be the one out front…that's the kind of soldier he was.

In less than twenty minutes, the radioman came back with "all clear." The medivac folks were moving in now to pick up the casualties. The marine snipers went on "high alert," knowing that the enemy might still be entrenched and would want to take out a chopper with stolen handheld missiles. It was protocol that details were seldom relayed over radios or cell phones and then, only code or slang. The insurgents had the capabilities to intercept and many of them could speak English.

The platoon reorganized and set in motion to return to base. The medivac chopper set down within minutes, carrying away two soldiers. The base triage people went to work and saw immediately that one soldier was beyond help, but the other had a good chance of making it with a scalp wound. Neither of the soldiers was Andre. The injured soldier managed to say, "Three or four more guys are hurt. They're coming back in the humvees."

Constantine went to the staging area and waited for the ambushed platoon to return. When he heard the roar of their engines, he saw that his son was driving the front vehicle, with the lieutenant in the passenger's seat with both arms bandaged. The triage crew went back to work and three more soldiers were admitted to the hospital, all appearing to be survivors. When Andre was explaining the incident to the commander and Constantine, he faltered and started to fall, and he mumbled, his adrenaline-high dissipated, "Oh yeah, I'm hit somewhere on my butt." They caught him before he hit the deck, and noticed he was bleeding through his uniform trousers.

There were several medics checking out the returning soldiers and when they saw Andre collapse, they quickly placed him a litter and got him to the ER. His wound turned out to be superficial through his right butt cheek, just a lot of blood being pumped by an excited heart.

When Andre was relaxed on the hospital bed and lying on his belly, with his bandaged butt exposed, swollen and bruised, Constantine said, "You had to go and get a Purple Heart. I promised your mother that you would be safe and sound. Plus, I heard through the lieutenant that you might be up for a Bronze Star for the way you took the fight to the enemy. Mother will not be happy with me…but very proud of you."

"I couldn't help myself. The bastards got me so mad. They'll never stand toe-to-toe and fight. They're just sneaky, cowardly pukes. They shot Raoul first. He's my friend from New York – a real good man trying to help. The kids love that guy. He never had a chance."

Constantine patted him lightly on the shoulder and asserted, "God will sort them out. Raoul will get through the Pearly Gates." He then told him all about his grandfather, and the plans to return to Yap.

"Sure, I'll go. I want to see Grandpa for Christmas. Maybe we'll celebrate our birthdays too. If I know Auntie Ericka, she's already planning a bunch of parties and fiestas on the beach."

"Oh yeah! We'll have to check with the doc and see when you can travel. Sitting will be a problem for awhile. We'll get you one of those air-filled seat donuts."

Andre smiled and then drifted off to sleep. The drugs were working their magic.

The medical records and letters from John's doctor and wife Anna showed on the email without a hitch. During the night, Constantine filled out the leave forms in preparation for the meeting with the commander next day.

At the meeting, the commanders said, "My aide already filled me in, and I looked at your service records. Both of you are on your second tour and both are recommended for re-upping if you decide to. Constantine, you are over half-way to your retirement. You should hang in for another eight to ten years."

"I'll probably re-enlist. I don't know about Andre. He's got his eye on a little sweetie for a life on Saipan. He may want to go home and start a family."

"We'll talk about that sometime in the future. I've already signed all the paperwork for your leaves. You'll be gone for six weeks. If you need longer, you know where you can find me. I've got another eight months on this hitch, and then I have to make some decisions. My family wants me to come home. They're always worried about me getting blown up."

"Sir, not going to happen. You're tougher than shoe leather and meaner than a snake. Besides, you've got a lot of retirement to collect!"

"Hoo-rah! Go see your islands, Soldier."

The doctor wanted Andre to stay a few more days just to make sure that an infection didn't set in. Meanwhile, Constantine got their gear organized and much of their personal belongings, he shipped home to Yap via the US Post Office. He checked in the military equipment with the quartermaster. It felt strange not to wearing a helmet constantly and not carrying his rifle.

Both Constantine and Andre attended the battalion's memorial service for Raoul, before his remains were shipped home. This was clearly a band of brothers, working and living together, and facing a common threat. Many of the tough old non-coms broke out in tears. To them, losing a young vital man like Raoul, was like losing a son and a part of their family. The commander lauded Raoul and the many soldiers like him that protected freedom and democracy and kept the American borders safe from violence and tyranny.

After the doctor's clearance next day, Constantine and Andre boarded a commercial jet to Washington, D.C., and after an overnight, on to Los Angeles, Honolulu, Guam and then finally Yap. It would be a long two days. Thank goodness, the lads in Andre's platoon had fixed him with a lot of padding and even a children's bright green pool toy for his aching backside.

Constantine was thinking to himself, "How in the hell am I going to explain to Andre's mother, Belle, that he managed to get him injured? Fighting armed insurgents was one thing – facing an angry mother was quite another matter."

Chapter 6

HELEN ON THE MAINLAND

Being second born and the first girl, Helen was the dynamic, most energetic, and probably the favorite in the family. She was always solving problems and looking over the horizon for the next adventure. From an early age, John and Anna knew there was no keeping Helen on the island in a traditional family life. She was never interested in the island boys, knowing that if she stayed, she'd would grow up, be a wife and mother, and never have a chance to follow her dreams.

When several Peace Corps volunteers came to the island to teach English and math, she enrolled in all the classes, wanting to improve and be prepared for the Big World. Little did she suspect that she would fall in love and maybe re-consider her role as wife and mother, but definitely not on her small island. A bright young man from Oregon, Ronnie Thompson, caught her eye…and vice-versa. She viewed him as handsome beyond words, and he always told her, "You have the widest, prettiest smile in all of Micronesia." The two became inseparable and sometimes, Helen would take the same classes two or three times, just so she could talk to Ronnie.

Ronnie had graduated from the University of Oregon with a degree in language arts. He wanted to be a writer, but worked in the Peace Corps as teacher to pay his bills and to learn about life. Helen noticed that he was always making notes and writing down interesting passages that he found in his readings. When she told him about the Great Pacific Northwest, she pulled out her atlas and also contacted the financial aids counselor at the local college. She knew she wanted to go to the University of Oregon to study sociology and maybe become a teacher or researcher; and if Ronnie returned to the university to work on his Master's Degree, it would even be better than she imagined.

Ronnie was on a two-year contract with the Peace Corps. During this time, he met with John and Anna, and he was accepted into the family. Ronnie's contract ended about the time Helen graduated from high school and turned eighteen, and they made plans to go to the University. Not wanting to rush into marriage, John and Anna agreed that she could go, as long as she lived in the women's dorm, and used good sense in her relationship with Ronnie. Ronnie left several weeks before her departure, trying to sell one of his short stories in Seattle.

When she left, the airport send-off for Helen was spectacular, even for the islands. The elders knew that she would do well, being bright and poised, and that she would be good role model about the Yapese. A lot of people vicariously pinned their hopes and dreams on the college students. Many of the elders had wanted to make a move but never developed the courage or had the resources.

Ronnie sold his story and picked up a few bucks for their living expenses. He sold several more in the following months and was on his way to earning a living as a writer, which was unusual for new, struggling writers. The couple combined their student loans, rented a small apartment near the university, and got by with only one car. Babies were not in their plans, but travel was. During breaks, they hopped buses and saw the entire country with their month-long bus pass during the summer break. They rode into Canada several times, and on each trip, Ronnie picked up ideas and materials for his stories, while Helen was becoming an ace photographer. Her photos often sold with Ronnie's stories.

Helen's parents made several trips to the mainland, mainly for attending conferences in education or art. John was now a full-fledged, respected teacher and Anna was becoming noted for his art, and her weavings were selling briskly throughout the USA and Europe. She also developed a market for the carvers from Yap and Chuuk. Their carvings from mangrove wood of warriors, sharks and masks were in demand, and were of museum quality.

Every time Anna met with Helen or talked to her on the phone, the subject of marriage always came up, as did the baby situation. When she could, she changed the subject, and never mentioned the whole idea of being tied down with one person to Ronnie. She knew he was free spirit and wasn't into traditions like having a nuclear family and moving to the suburbs. Helen enjoyed being with Ronnie and didn't want to scare him away. Ronnie didn't seem to care about other women for romance and commitment. But lately, Helen couldn't explain, even to herself, that she felt her biological clock starting to tick and the family traditions about marriage and children kept popping to the surface.

After a long trip to the Grand Canyon, and they were freshly showered and curled up in their warm, cozy bed, Helen finally worked up her nerve, and asked Ronnie how he felt about marriage. He smiled and said, "Thought you'd never ask. I was afraid to talk about it because I knew you wanted to be free and experience life on your own terms…so I never brought it up. How do I feel? Simply put, I love you and you know it. I'll leave the marriage thing up to you, but just so you know, if you wanted to get married, I would jump at a chance for a lifetime with you."

"I love you, too."

"I know it sounds corny and it's probably over-used, but I feel like we're soul mates, that we've been together forever. Maybe even in a former lifetime. I enjoy being with you. Sometimes we think so much alike, or anticipate each other's thought, that it seems like *déjà vu*, like we done this before and probably together."

"Then why don't you propose? Don't you wanna know my answer?"

"Hang on. I wanna do this right. I'm going to find one of my cigars."

He fumbled around in a desk drawer and found his five-pack of cigars. He took the band off one of the cigars, dropped to one knee, looked into Helen's eyes and asked, "Will you marry me, a struggling writer with money one day and broke the next? I'll never be able to do a nine-to-five job, but I'll work hard to support you and our babies if it happens."

"Sure I'll marry you. I'll want some bambinos some day."

With that, he slipped the cigar band on her marriage finger and said, "I pronounce you officially engaged. You're my fiancée and vice-versa."

She exclaimed, "We've got to celebrate. Should we call your parents? My parents are so used to you and me together, that I think they'll say 'congratulations' and fall back to sleep."

"My mother always said I should marry you before some other galoot stole you away."

"Let's not call my parents until we graduate next month; but I think we should get married right away, maybe drive over to Reno next weekend for a quickie Nevada marriage. I'd appreciate the official, written commitment."

"Works for me, my little Cutie Fiancée." They soon fell asleep with contented smiles on their faces.

The trip to Reno was romantic and fun. They held hands most of the way and reminisced about their courting years. The civil ceremony was nice and sweet with lots of flowers and champagne. They bought simple gold bands to complete the ceremony. It was an eventful fast weekend. Both had to get back to their college classes, and Ronnie was doing research for a story on global warming and the impact on the tiny atoll islands in the Pacific.

The call from Anna about John's condition came the following evening. When Ronnie walked in the door, Helen was just putting down the phone. She looked worried, even a little scared. She told him about her father and his failing heart, and what his plans were for Christmas.

He hugged her and massaged her forehead, "Christmas is certainly going to be bittersweet this year. It'll be good to see everyone. Maybe

all the family and excitement, and the Christmas feelings and sentiments, will help your father to stay around longer."

"I hope so. I love that old man."

Chapter 7

CHRISTMAS ON YAP

O ver two thousand years, a baby was born in Bethlehem through immaculate conception to a couple from Nazareth, Joseph and Mary. There was no room at the inn, so the couple were forced to stay in the manger with farm animals. Jesus was born and Mary placed him in a warm bed of straw and blankets. His name was Jesus Christ and he was the Son of God, and was to go on and spread the gospel of Christianity until he was eventually put to death by crucifixion *cruci figo* at age thirty-three at the hands of the Roman Conquerors and part of a conspiracy with the Jewish religious leaders. Jews had been expecting Christ (the Messiah) but because their expectations did not match the person and methods of Jesus, they rejected him as the true Messiah. He was also unpopular for wanting to stop prostitution and gambling, and being involved in general religious matters where the priests considered themselves the absolute authority.

At least what we've been taught. Biblical research has shown that no one knows exactly when Christ was born and it might well not be December 25 – as the activities described in conjunction with the event are associated with spring, not winter. Nor did Christians celebrate Christ's birth when the religion was new. It wasn't until about the 3rd Century A.D. that December 25 was categorized as a holy day by the Church. Apparently one of the reasons that the Christian fathers set such a date was they were trying to compete with another growing religion, *Mithraism* – the worship of the sun god – whose big day was also December 25.

Of course, we know Jesus' strong message was one of love, peace and forgiveness, and showed the way to Heaven through the glory of God. In Christianity, he is considered the true Savior of the world. Christ is the Greek word for the Hebrew word Messiah.

Jesus' messages never died, much of what he taught is contained in the Bible (for example, the Books of Mark, Matthew, Acts, etc.). It is still the top seller of all books ever printed. The Spanish brought Christianity to the Micronesian Islands and to the Philippines, and peoples celebrate Christmas every year on December 25 to commemorate the birth of Christ. The Philippines is still the only primarily Christian nation in Asia, being over ninety percent Catholic. Both being former Spanish colonies, there is still a great deal of interaction and trade between the Philippines and Micronesia.

Christmas is a major holiday in Yap and the surrounding islands. It is warm and tropical along the equator, thus the banana tree or giant fern are substituted for the evergreen spruce tree that the mainland expects. The local trees are decorated with multi-colored lights and homemade ornaments, and take a center place in the main living room. Gift giving is every bit as important and under the tree, the children will expect to find gaily wrapped, colorful presents. Houses and huts are often outlined with strings of lights and oftentimes, there'll be a large star on the rooftop. The school plays all have the manger story, and the shepherds being alerted by the angels and the three wise men bearing gifts for Baby Jesus.

The island children also know the history of Santa through their school studies and the internet. The first Santa was the Bishop of Myra of Asia Minor, St. Nicholas, who today remains a principal saint of the Eastern Orthodox Church, which had broken off from the Roman Catholic Church. In the 4th Century, he distributed presents to good children on his feast day, December 6.

The tradition of hanging stockings on the mantel to receive small gifts originated with the Turkish version of St. Nicholas. Long ago,

St. Nick was supposed to have provided dowries for the three lonely daughters of a poor nobleman. He threw bags of money through their windows (in another version down the chimney), where the gifts happened to fall into a stocking that was hung by the fire to dry.

During the Protestant Reformation, St. Nicholas was replaced in many countries by the Christmas Man, known in England as Father Christmas and in France as Pere Noel. In the Netherlands, where St. Nicholas was the patron saint of sailors, he was extremely popular and was known as *Sint Nicholas* or *Sinterclaas*, and the Dutch children expected him to leave candies and presents in their wooden clogs on his feast day. Both this tradition and the name were Americanized and Sinterclaas became Santa Claus.

The children know about Santa Claus and they look forward to his visits in his canoe filled with gifts and toys. There's no mantel to hang stockings, which they don't own when they wear sandals all the time, so they decorate pillow cases and hang them anywhere for the night-time goodies. Santa often comes in darkness when it's cool and the children are asleep. While he's in the tropics, Santa tends to be lightly dressed in an aloha shirt and red surfer shorts. He does maintain his red hat with a big white ball on the end, but flip-flops are substituted for his shiny black boots. He's a roly-poly large man with brown skin, and likes to say "Ho-ho-ho!" The children get a little confused because usually Santa is portrayed as a white man, but it was easily explained that he gets real tanned as he nears the equator. The children knew that the bright sun either made a white person sunburned or tanned, so they readily accepted the explanation that Santa's skin just darkens up.

Sometimes, Santa visits the supply and grocery shops, and just like in the big department stores on the mainland, sits and talks to the children, and take requests for their Christmas wishes. The children love his big white fluffy beard and his large handle-bar mustache. Carolers are apt to show up and sing all the Christmas favorite hymns when Santa is in town. One of the favorites is "Silent Night." They sing the carols in both English and Yapese.

CHRISTMAS IN THE TROPICS

It seems a little unusual to hear the songs "I Saw Mama Kissing Santa Claus Last Night," "Chestnuts Roasting on An Open Fire" or "Rudolph, the Red-Nosed Reindeer" coming out of the boom-boxes, but it's all done in the spirit and best traditions of Christmas, and the island children usually have parents that have been to the main-land, and most of them are in a family that own a DVD player with Christmas movies. Christmas cards are seldom posted, but if there are cards in the stationery store, then the cards will be delivered personally from house to house. Oftentimes, the children will make their own Christmas cards and holiday decorations. Children also write letters to Santa at a faraway place called the North Pole.

Chapter 8

FINDING EDUARDO

Eduardo was the third child born to John and Anna. It was immediately noticed that he was handsome and brilliant beyond his years, but he was restless, non-focused and seemed continually anxious and nervous. He was immature for whatever age he happened to be. He was mischievous and often broke the family rules, driving his father John into rages and anger that he had never experienced in his entire life. Eduardo would go off swimming without a buddy to watch over him; he was often late for dinner and not doing his homework; and sometimes he talked back to his mother, and on several occasions, he was insulting. The parents were more than patient and spoke to him on every violation and imposed discipline, trying to come to the root cause of his poor behavior. The village priest had him in his office a dozen times, as did the school principal.

The islands are sadly lacking for professional family and school counselors. The little money available is needed for school equipment and supplies, and meager teacher's salaries. Thus, year after year, Eduardo went without personal, direct counseling, and he found himself with the losers of the islands, drop-out types and youngsters experimenting with everything from betel nut and alcohol to marijuana. There were no parenting classes so that John and Anna could learn coping skills and offset their fears that they were facing as parents. No one had ever told them about boundaries and expectations, and they blamed much of Eduardo's deficiencies on themselves. They had no concept of the "bad seed" child or realizing that much of Eduardo's emotional growth and progress would depend on him completely.

John found him drunk several times on the beach, and Anna was frantic about what would happen to him. His older siblings tried talking some sense into him, gave him support and love, but nothing seemed to work. Constantine even kicked him in the buttocks on one occasion and told him he was "a stupid shit." They didn't know that there is a gene that makes one pre-disposed to alcoholism and that probably he had a strong allergic reaction to alcohol and certain drugs. He had no medical tests and was obviously wired for falling under the spell of substance abuse and chemical dependency. Sometimes these misfits are just written off by families and society.

He even started the 'visiting different doctors' routine and got hooked on prescription drugs, some to get him up, calm him down and sometimes trying to find a balance. But Eduardo wasn't interested in any kind of balance. He abused all the legitimate drugs, fabricating and counterfeiting prescription slips as he went along and of course, making the doctors realize they had a druggie in their offices. He started on some injectables during this period.

Eduardo was a classic example of arrested development. There was something inescapably embarrassing about him to the family and to the island. He started listening to acid rock and applying amateurish tattoos at an early age, and upon reaching early adulthood, was still listening to the same music, wearing the same clothes, still finding space on his arms for yet another tattoo, and still playing the isolated anti-hero. He didn't now how to maneuver or paddle a canoe.

Finally when he was eighteen and had obtained a passport, he was off to Guam and then onto California. John and Anna couldn't figure out where he got the money, but there was gossip that he was seen loading marijuana onto visiting yachts. Each step in his wayward life, he managed to attract the attention of the police, and by the time he left Guam, there were three cases pending against him, dealing with traffic violations, narcotics possession and petty theft. Without some guidance, he was headed for a serious meltdown. He was destined to go to jail and if he didn't change his behavior, he would likely end up being involved in serious, violent crimes and probably prison; and what happens with druggies, he would be found overdosed or frozen to death on a skid row in some large city. His early cute Peter Pan syndrome was not working any more. Even his fellow dopers were tired of his act and his moochiness.

No one in the family heard from him for several years. He was the prodigal son. Occasionally he would send his mother a birthday card, and even on one occasion, he mailed her a pair of diamond earrings. Anna was concerned that the jewelry was the proceeds of some criminal activity and didn't wear them, thinking of bad karma. She hid them away in a metal box where she kept all her important papers and photos, in a water-tight metal box buried in the sand next to the house.

Constantine checked his name against all the web search sites and found that he was living near Los Angeles and working for a computer company. A magazine article said that he had invented intriguing software for a game company and that his ideas had made the characters in the games more realistic. Unfortunately when he called the computer company, he found that Eduardo had been discharged and was confidentially told that Eduardo had become a heroin addict, and that he needed professional and family help. He gave Constantine his last known address. When Constantine went to the address on one of his Army leaves, the landlord told him that Eduardo had checked out without any forwarding address and had not paid the rent.

About two years later, Helen received a weird phone call from an adult male that sounded drunk or mentally ill. After she talked to him for awhile, she determined that it was Eduardo and he was definitely falling off the deep end. He had found Helen through one of Ronnie's magazine articles and her photos. He said that he was in Washington and would like to come south for a visit. He said that he had been living on the street close to physical and mental dysfunctional, panhandling for wine and was ill, probably with tuberculosis.

CHRISTMAS IN THE TROPICS

Helen told him to hold off until he spoke to Ronnie. There was no way that she was going to bring a drunk, sick person into their house, now that she was pregnant with their second child. It didn't matter to her that he was her brother – she had told him a long time ago to choose between alcohol and drugs, or the family. He went the wrong way in life and so be it.

Ronnie, being the kind person that he was, said that he would meet with Eduardo and see what they could do to get him back on track. He wasn't going to have him in the house with a communicable disease, but was willing to get him to the general hospital and a shelter until he got his act together. Eduardo called the next day and spoke to Ronnie. He agreed to hitchhike south and head for the Golden Temple Shelter in downtown Portland. He called two days later, and said that he was at the shelter and that a volunteer doctor was working on the cough and lung problems. Ronnie said that he would meet with him about eight o'clock that evening.

When they met, Ronnie couldn't believe the beat-up, washed-out appearance of Eduardo. He had been a strapping young man with a six-pack belly with a chestnut brown, happy face. What he saw was a walking skeleton and close to a deathly white, pale out-of-shape man who was nearly thirty years old chronologically but now looked closer to fifty. He face was gaunt and he had lost several teeth, either from bar fighting or from too much betel nut.

"I know, I look like a bucket of feces. I can tell by your face, the way you're looking at me." His eyes had nervous twitches and he coughed several times.

"I'm not the kind of guy that says 'I told you so,' but I remember like it was yesterday when we warned you about dope and booze, and all you could say was

'Buzz off!' Now you've hit bottom, are you ready for detox and getting it back together? You've still gotta lot of life left if you protect your health. Are you off the opiates?"

"Yeah Ron, I'm on bottom but I did beat heroin. I couldn't afford it anymore. I'm a wino …a low-life bum. I spent a coupla winters in the Oregon snow. I thought I was going to die."

"Probably accounts for your pneumonia or TB. Right now, I can't have you around Helen and our baby, and we've got another on the way. I'm not going to jeopardize them in any way. You can talk on the phone. Helen wants to tell you about your Dad. He's pretty sick."

"What's the problem? I thought that old man would live forever."

Ronnie filled him in on what he knew, and said to call Helen tomorrow afternoon for the details. He told him about the planned reunion at Christmas, and that by then, he should be healthy enough, and not contagious, to travel. Before he left, Ronnie talked to the volunteer doctor and the shelter counselor. Both of them felt that Eduardo was sincere about recovering from his abusive life-style; and that he might have a chance.

Next day, Eduardo and Helen talked for several hours on the phone. She also spoke to his doctor and his counselor, and some of the shelter workers. There was a consensus that Eduardo was on the way back and he appeared strong enough mentally not to relapse. The counselor told Helen that Eduardo had hit bottom hard, hard enough that it knocked some sense into him. Eduardo told him that when he couldn't breath, in that moment a light finally went on that he realized that he could die early. The doctor said that Eduardo was already improving with several doses of anti-biotic, just staying warm, and eating some nutritional food. Helen told Eduardo that she and Ronnie would help him with an airplane ticket, no cash though, to get him home in about a month if he stayed sober.

When Ronnie arrived home, Helen guided him to an overhanging sprig of mistletoe. She said, "I've been waiting to kiss my favorite husband. You are one of a kind. You're even more dashing than Sir Lancelot and more prestigious than Dr. Schweitzer. Thank you so much for helping my brother." They kissed and hugged.

CHRISTMAS IN THE TROPICS

"Hey, when I married you, I married your family…and when we arrive home in Ulithi, you being a favorite home-girl, it'll be apparent real fast that I married the entire village."

Helen laughed, "Yep, that's right. You'll always have a friend or two…or maybe a dozen or more. Remember to bring lots of rice and chicken."

Chapter 9

JOHN BACK HOME ON HIS ISLAND

John and Anna, and the rest of the family arrived home on Ulithi safe and sound. There were a few strong winds but nothing to throw them off course or get everyone seasick. Once John saw his island on the horizon, he felt relieved and happy that he managed to get home. He actually felt stronger – maybe it was the medication or the good nutrition, or bursts of adrenaline, or maybe it was just being home for Christmas and seeing all his friends. Family members had already cleaned and prepared their home and had fresh linen in the bedroom, and it appeared that there were tons of fresh fruit. John would be ecstatic when spotted his favorite green, but ripe, tangerines laying in the shade in their outside kitchen area.

John's home area of Ulithi consisted of about one thousand people and was actually 106 miles northeast of Yap Proper with forty-nine islets on its reef which encloses a 183-square-mile lagoon. The early Jesuits got there in 1731 under Father Juan Antonio Cantova but were soon wiped out by the local islanders. The Japanese colonists had built an airstrip but when the American bombing started, they retreated to Yap Proper. On September 29, 1944, the United States Navy occupied Ulithi unopposed. Subsequently a thousand US warships assembled in the lagoon prior to moving north and then making landings on Iwo Jima and Okinawa.

CHRISTMAS IN THE TROPICS

The Micronesian field trip ships calls at Ulithi on it outward and inward journeys, dropping off supplies and providing medical services. If a life-and-death emergency developed, Anna could always call on the Pacific Missionary Aviation (PMA) to either bring out emergency medical personnel and medicines, and/or take the patient to the main Yap hospital.

With just a little help, John managed to step from the boat and walk up the beach to the island community. It felt sensational for his feet to tread once again on the public walkway. He knew the paths were well-engineered with stones holding up the edges and a system of culverts allowing drainage but not erosion. The paths had stayed in place for centuries with only minimal upkeep. His walking stick was perfect for keeping his balance, and many of his friends made comments about the designing skill and creativity of the cane carver. When John spotted his house with the fresh coat of paint, he started to tear up and slowed his walk. Anna took him by the arm and guided him up from the beach walkway to the front door of their home.

He said, "It's so good to be home again. I needed to be here –on the sea of tranquility. I've got to get out of this western clothing. Where's my thu."

"In time, my Sweet Man. Let's get you into the bedroom so you can change. Ericka and her friends have everything so nice and clean, and organized."

John quipped. "So nice and organized that I won't be able to find anything."

"Not to worry. Erica knows where you like to keep your 'stuff.' The bedroom looks good and spacious for you to maneuver. She's found you an old wheelchair if you think you need one."

"No wheelchair yet, but it might come to that. The doctor said I would gradually weaken. The heart will keep pumping but won't be real efficient for carrying oxygen and promoting energy."

Anna smiled, "We'll talk all about that later. Just relax for about two hours, then the community has a feast planned for you."

John slipped out of his clothes and literally, almost fell into the fluffy sheets, naked and free like a child.

Looking out the window towards the beach with the lagoon a dozen shades of blue and green, he thought back to his childhood days, running and splashing through the surf. He remembered his father and uncles taking him fishing and teaching him to be quiet and patient, and learning to respect the reef as the lifeblood of food for the village. His father explained the balance of nature and how all life depended on the interaction of other life forms. He thought about his father taking him to the *pebai* to discuss community issues and problems, and then into the nearby *faluw*, the men's house. He guffawed softly to himself about how he always wondered what went on in the *dapal*, the women's house. He had heard that the women often went there when they were in their monthly cycle, or when they wanted to complain about their husbands.

When he was thirteen, his father had given him his first piece of *rai*, the large donut-shaped wheel money that was quarried from Palau originally. The former Japanese colonists had once counted 13,281 pieces of stone money on the Yap Islands and about half of them still survive into the 21st Century. The value of the "large coin" comes from tradition and negotiation, and also how it was brought to Yap by Captain David Dean O'Keefe formerly of Savannah, Georgia. He is often referred to as the "Tattooed Irishman," and he transported the rai from the mine on Palau on his Chinese junk across hundreds of miles on a perilous sea. Almost every village in Yap has stone money on display, mostly on private land, and it's seldom moved because it's common knowledge who owns each piece of rai. The "hard currency" money resembles a flat gristmill with a hole in the middle, so two or more men can carry it on a pole. There are exceptions about how many men can move a piece of the coin. A rai on Rumung is so large that it takes at least twelve men to lift and carry it. Another large coin, over eight feet in diameter, is in the village of Kadaay.

John thought back about his first rai. It only weighed about one hundred pounds, but it was all his. When his father died, he and his siblings inherited another fourteen pieces, and they all agreed that the stones would be mutually owned by all family members. This avoided the arguments about parental possessions after any death. John still had five pieces on display on his property, and when he passed, the rai would be commonly owned by his four offspring. He was forever chasing little children from the rai, as the village decided that sitting or standing on stone money is forbidden. The money is considered sacred to Yap's history. By written law, it definitely cannot be removed from Yap.

Anna woke him from his reverie, half sleep and the other half filled with dreams and memories. It felt good to dress in his blue thu, a long cloth wrapped around his waist and up between his legs, and he was ready to see his friends and eat some excellent local, healthy food. John took his place at the head of the table and all his friends and relatives passed by with greetings of "aloha" and wishing him a long life. The slight breeze blew away even the most ravenous mosquitoes. After an hour, Anna brought him a plate of vegetables and fruit, and a small piece of fish and a smaller piece of chicken with no skin. He noticed that she had also prepared *voi,* his favorite chestnut for additional protein.

He couldn't help himself and said, "If I keep eating all this vegetables, I'm going go turn into a rabbit. Man is a carnivore that needs plenty of meat. Where's the beef?"

Anna exclaimed, "I've always liked bunny rabbits. Better that than a dead dog!"

"Got me there, Pretty Woman. Besides, I've heard that rabbits can have a lot of fun."

"You heard right. Now chump on that good food, so you'll have plenty of energy. I think you're going to need it."

After the meal and few speeches, the visiting padre discussed leading a good life and reaping the rewards in the afterlife. John agreed with everything the man said, always believing in the Golden Rule and creating good karma throughout your life. Suddenly there was a banging of drums and the young people took center stage with a variety of wild and exciting dances. They were wearing tropical flowers, homemade oyster-shell necklaces, and bamboo strips as wrist bands, and did a combination of warlike stick dances and slow graceful dances like the Hawaiian hula. On some of the dances, they were standing and jumping, while others they sat cross-legged in front of John, banging pieces of bamboo in an ancient rhythm.

John clapped his hands in appreciation and chanted out loud on some the particularly hostile war dances. The drummers kept everything moving at a fun, exciting pace, especially in the loud war dances. He and Anna had done the same dances while they were younger, and the dance movements had passed from generation to generation, telling the stories of ancient warfare and heroism, and in many cases, about love and romance. They had always been a peaceful, defensive people, but would fight if their families or land were threatened. Family was of paramount importance.

In appreciation of the cycle of life, John watched the seabirds scooting back and forth along the shore as the waves came in and broke, and spread pieces of tiny debris all over the sandy beach. He knew the birds were finding things to eat from the roiling surf. He observed the larger birds, probably egrets, swooping and diving on the horizon. He wished there were more swallows on the island eating mosquitoes and any insects that fell victim to their voracious appetites.

After traveling for almost three days from Hawaii to Guam, then Yap Proper on and on by boat to home, John was fatigued and asked Anna to help him to bed. He was too weary to shower so Anna gave him a quick, refreshing sponge bath. He took his medication and drifted off to a long, healthy sleep.

He dreamed off and on about his college and teaching days, but mostly he thought of splendid days walking under a canopy of banyan trees hand-in-hand with Anna, his beautiful bride. He thought himself so loved and so fortunate.

The Christmas Season made everything so real for him...family, friends and good tidings. What else did a man need? He chuckled to himself, "A new heart would be good."

Chapter 10

OUT OF IRAQ

It wasn't easy for Constantine and Andre to get out of Iraq. Andre developed a low-grade infection in his buttocks and some of the paperwork from John's doctor was lost between the fax machine and the general's clerk. Constantine summarized, "Andre, look at it this way. Nothing worthwhile is routine and easy. We're in a faraway country and part of a bureaucratic nightmare, called the military."

Fortunately, the whole shebang was organized three days later, and Andre was well enough to travel. Constantine confirmed the flights and layovers. He called Anna and said they would be several days later, but not to worry. They were coming for sure, and the general told them if they needed more than six weeks to let him know. Both men received exemplary evaluation reports from their supervisors, and both were recommended for re-enlistment if they so chose. Trying to keep the ranks full with a volunteer army is not easy. Both men were offered hefty bonuses to stay in, and their future educational benefits were doubled.

The medics set Andre with a special flight bed on an Air Force plane bound for Texas. From there, they would start traveling home on Continental Airlines flying out of Houston. Continental Airlines was one of the few planes that landed in Guam, and the only one to go all the way to Yap.

Andre was fighting a mental and emotional struggle about re-enlistment. He enjoyed much of the military life, but he was mainly thinking of a girl that he had met in Fort Jackson during their training sessions. She was lithesome, gung-ho, athletic, sexy young woman from Tennessee. There were not enough adjectives in the English languages to define how he would describe her or how he cherished her. They were both due to get out of the Army in four months, and she would have much to do with his future plans. Right now, she was stationed in Germany as a computer analysis expert. Her name was Vicky Pate and she could trace her lineage back to Daniel Boone and the early explorers.

When he told her over the phone about his wound, Vicky said, being relieved the injury was minor, "Maybe we should get out before you're injured badly or end up with a free gravestone at the military cemetery. We've got to be serious about this. It could happen."

"When you say 'we,' are you saying what I think you're saying."

"Hey, we talked about this. We're a team, a couple, love buddies, bed-mates, etc. I'll follow you anywhere."

"How about to the altar? We could look at a lifetime commitment. It can work. My parents have been married forever."

"Yeah, we talked about this also. I have to make a decision about us in the next few months. If I re-enlist, I'll be rotated back to Iraq again, or maybe Afghanistan."

Andre continued, "Too frigging dangerous. Get ready for this." He lowered his voice and asked, "Vicky Pate, will you marry me?

"Of course I will, you Big Hombre. A wedding proposal to a gal in Germany and you're in Iraq, and the telephone call being paid for the US Government. What a deal! Love this modern technology."

"We'll start planning. I'll tell Papa Constantine that his boy is not re-enlisting and is planning a spring wedding."

"Remember part of our deal, what we talked about?"

"Yeah, sure do. I'm with you. We go to college and you don't get locked down on a remote island. Most of our young island people end up moving away because there's no jobs and it gets real boring after awhile. I don't see myself fishing or growing taro and coconuts for the next fifty years."

She laughed and said, "It might be good to go for a visit. It looks so beautiful in your islands."

"Moon light walks on the beach are unforgettable.'

"Then, go tell your father that we're officially engaged. None of my friends will be surprised – I've got your photos all over my wall in the dorm. I'll let the First Sergeant know about my plans. He'll be pushing tons of bennies to get me to stay in. One of my colleagues just re-enlisted. The sarge got her on the patriotism angle, like how can you leave the Army when we're still at war on two fronts!"

"We're doing this together so let don't them persuade you to stay during a moment of weakness."

"Ain't going to happen. Go tell your father. I hope your mother will approve. I already told you that my parents approved after I sent them a bunch of photos and we did that video tape the last time you were on leave."

"My mom will approve. If she knows you're going to college and will have her grandbabies one day, then you'll be home free."

After the call, he found his father Constantine back in the barracks doing the final packing. The paperwork was finished and everything confirmed. They were hoping to get out by dark. If the insurgent's missile attacks hit, it was usually at nighttime. Then everything got shut down, responses organized and the wounded taken care of by responding medics. So far, so good. They actually saw their troop carrier plane warming up on the field and the flight crew doing the final checks.

Constantine was happy to hear about Vicky. He had met her twice and she seemed like a nice young lady, squared away, and respectful. His wife, Belle, would like that, especially the part about going to college.

Belle had been living on Guam in the military housing for families. She had made many friends, joined a number of support agencies, at-tended college, and did a lot of shopping with her nearby sister. As he and Andre rounded up their gear to head home from Iraq, he was still trying out the best way to tell his wife about Andre being wounded. When they agreed that he could go in the Army and skip college for a few years, Constantine promised to watch over him. He had talked to her on the phone about his father and the reunion on Yap, but hadn't mentioned anything about Andre, except that Andre got a humanitarian leave also.

Andre moved into special bed on the plane, making it easy to find a comfortable spot for his backside. Constantine knew that the front line lieutenant has recommended Andre for a Purple Heart and a Bronze Star for bravery, and figured the medals would be forthcoming at a military ceremony on Guam sometime in the future. He had read the paperwork, and could see from the obvious facts that Andre had gone way past a regular response to the enemy. He had acted like a bonifide hero, confronting the enemy head-on and probably helping to save the lives of his fellow soldiers. The lieutenant said that he had been shot in both arms, and that if Andre hadn't come to his aid, he would probably have been overrun by the enemy.

Constantine looked over at his son, now a full man and a credit to the Army. He felt proud, knowing that he and Belle had raised a little island boy that had transposed into a respectful man. Now he was moving into the next generation, deciding to take on a wife and maybe start a family. He figured he would start off slowly with Belle and talk about the good things that had happened with Andre, and hold off on the information that he had been shot in the butt.

The flight to the air force base in Texas was smooth and uneventful. They over-nighted in the BOQ (Bachelor Officer's Quarters) and arrived next morning at the international airport for their commercial flight to Honolulu. Andre had bought a blow-up ring for his backside, which cushioned perfectly. When the crew found out that they were returning soldiers from Iraq, they were moved up to first class and enjoyed steaks and champagne for their eight hour flight. The flight attendants flirted mercilessly with Andre until he started talking about his fiancée Vicky. They didn't bother with Constantine – he was always wearing his wedding ring.

CHRISTMAS IN THE TROPICS

With just a few hours layover, the lads were on another long flight to Guam. Before he left, Constantine spoke to Belle. He told her that he had a big surprise for her, that he was bringing home a true warrior. Belle asked for hints, and tried to find out if it was Andre, but all Constantine said was that he would see her in eight hours. She said that she had the sister's SUV and that there would be plenty of room for them and their luggage. They planned on staying on Guam for several days before pushing on to Yap. Belle kept everyone informed in the islands about the two boys coming home to Ulithi.

On the next segment, they were put automatically into first class, thanks to the courtesy of the previous crew. The seats laid back almost like a lounge, and they both got a good rest before landing on Guam. Andre popped a combination sleeping and pain pill and was out for four hours. Constantine couldn't believe the luxury and managed to wolf down half of Andre's steak as well as his own. Two glasses of champagne sent him to slumberland for almost three hours.

After landing and getting through the immigration and customs counters, they spotted Belle and her sister, Leilani, just past the security entrance. The women ran over to the men and gave them giant hugs. As they pushed the cart towards the SUV, Belle noticed Andre limping and walking askew.

She looked at Constantine and said, "Is this the surprise. Our boy is hurt?"

"Our boy is a hero. He earned two medals just two weeks ago and probably saved a coupla lives after they were ambushed."

In his best corny response, Andre said, "Ah shucks, Dad. It weren't nothin'."

Belle lightly punched Constantine in the arm and exclaimed, "This wasn't part of our deal. Why was he sent out on a dangerous patrol?"

"Calm down. It's part of the job and he's a survivor. He'll heal up like new in a few weeks. Right now, he's just got a sore butt."

Leilani said, "Constantine is right. Everything turned out okay, and he's a hero. Calm down and be happy your boy is back."

Constantine interjected, "And that's not all. The next part will be told by Andre himself."

"Mom, steady yourself. I know how I always said I wouldn't get married until I was thirty, that I wanted to finish college and do some traveling. Well, that all changed when I met my sweet girl Vicky. She's from Tennessee and got the cutest, softest Southern accent. You'll love her."

"Is that the girl you mentioned in your emails? You sent me some pictures too."

"Yeah, that's her. She wants out of the Army just like I do, maybe in about four months. We'd like to get married in Micronesia but leave soon after for college, maybe live in Tennessee and get local tuition. Or if she wanted, we could go to the University of Guam and get in-state tuition based on my home in Yap."

Belle concluded, "Wow, this is a lot to absorb right away. I filled with such mixed emotions. Grandpa John is sick and that's very sad. Then my boy comes home a hero, shot-up, and wants to get married. And all this is magnified by my darling Constantine coming home safe and sound, and we get to curl up together tonight. What a roller coaster life."

Constantine said, "All of this made me think, life is so short and fragile, so maybe I should consider retiring in two years, rather than going for twenty-five years. I can go anytime after this hitch. I'll have almost twenty-two years in."

Belle said, "I like that idea. I'm just finishing up my counseling degree and can hang my shingle out next year as a certified family and marriage counselor. I would like to do that. We can bring our baby Sweetie back with us from Yap, now I'm almost finished college and you're leaving the Army and all its demands. You're a master mechanic, besides being an English teacher, maybe you could find a good job and we could live on Guam. This big island is kinda like a "baby Hawaii" with lots of advantages. It's between the mainland and the easy island life. We can hop down to Yap anytime or go vacationing in Asia. It's all very close and we've got our international airport."

Leilani summarized, "Hey, we could all end up on Guam. Andre and Vicky can definitely go to college here. If they decide on children, there's plenty of good hospitals and schools."

CHRISTMAS IN THE TROPICS

Andre laughed and said, "We can't go too fast on this thing. I don't even know if Vicky can stand the heat and humidity, or she can be so far from her parents and friends in Tennessee."

Constantine said, "And the sagas continue. There'll be another chapter tomorrow. Remember to tune in."

"Oh, we will. It's our story," answered Belle.

Chapter 11

"BABY GIRL" ERICA

W hereas Helen had always been the outgoing, popular girl in the family, Erica was the quiet one, a homebody who liked nothing better than to be cooking and cleaning and being with her mother and aunties. She enjoyed sitting around with the older ladies, drinking tea and talking about the island haps, including the gossip about who was buying too many material goods, or was wearing too much makeup, or who had a relationship and with whom. As a consequence, she was a great source of information about traditional values and traditions, passed from mother to daughter, and was a skilled dancer. She also was well-known for her recipes and cooking talents and her embroidery was often shown in prominence at island art shows.

When her mother and father were away, she was the head of household and kept things on track. Her parents didn't worry about anything; they knew Erica could take care of the house and all the problems associated with their grandchildren who were still on the island. It wasn't uncommon for a son or daughter to have offspring, then leave for the mainland for college or more opportunities, and leave their child with either maternal or paternal grandparents. Anna was raising a daughter, Sweetie, for Constantine and Belle, and a son, Andrew, for Eduardo who had impregnated the son's mother before he left for his life of drugs on the mainland

CHRISTMAS IN THE TROPICS

Erica didn't have a child or boyfriend or husband. Sometimes she became very lonely and often took to the beach walking alone, like she was floating on a cloud. Neighbors would see her, and comment, "Erica is out walking again. She might be dreaming up a boyfriend, maybe fantasizing about some faraway land."

Another neighbor would comment, "She's being a good daughter but she needs to think about her own life. She's wasting all her youth taking care of parents and nieces and nephews. Somebody should tell her to get on with her life. Get out see and experience the world. Maybe Constantine or Helen can talk some sense into her. The whole family will be together at Christmas."

Erica was indeed daydreaming about her life and what the future might bring. The family didn't know that she had had a boyfriend at one time, at least that's the way she perceived the relationship, with a handsome young man named Joey from the village of Maap. They had met in church and had clandestinely rendezvoused several times, once near her village and three other times in Colonia when her mother came in for shopping and to pay bills. They lightly kissed on their last contact, and he told he was going off to college and would write to her – but he never did. Erica saw his mother several times and asked how he was doing in college. The mother always answered the same, "He's doing fine. He is concentrating on his studies. He wants to be a doctor, maybe a surgeon."

Erica said, "I have a note for him. Could you send it to him with your next package?"

The mother answered, "Of course, I'll send your note. When we talk on the phone next, I will tell him you were asking about him."

She wrote several more notes and never heard back from the son. The mother always reassured her that she had sent the notes, and that he wasn't able to respond because he was so busy with his pre-medical program. When Erica asked for his address so she could write direct, the mother would become evasive, saying that she couldn't remember it, or Joey had moved and she hadn't received the new address. All Erica knew was that he was going to college somewhere in Oregon. Finally it hit her like a thunderbolt and she realized he could have written to her easily knowing her address on Ulithi. Five years had passed and she was still alone. She was angry about the whole situation, not so much at the son, but more at herself for being so naïve and planning on something that never really existed. The love affair happened in her mind and not in real life.

She knew that she had to make some major changes in her life, or she would end up stuck on the island. She was finished with her own rationalization that she had to stay on the island to help the family, to maintain the house, and after her father became sick, to keep their little farm going. She knew her mother wouldn't hold her back. She and her aunties had often said that she needed to go to college, or maybe travel, but to get off the rock with its provincial mindset. Her mother often said, "Think big. Have goals. Don't wait for life to come to you. Make it happen!" She chuckled to herself every time she thought of her mother's pep talk…and she also realized that her mother was clearly right.

Erica started making plans for the Christmas holidays. She would help with all the festivities and help her mother and her father have a memorable Christmas; but she also planned to talk to the other family members about some ideas about her future. She figured college was in her plans but had to decide what to study. She liked the idea of being a trained artist like her mother, and a teacher like her father. She wasn't interested in the military like Constantine and Andre, but she knew that she could get some wonderful insight about computer technology from her brother Eduardo with his creative ideas and also Belle, who did computer programming for several companies on Guam.

After her father arrived on island, she had everything humming and smooth like a well rehearsed symphony orchestra. She wanted her father to be comfortable and relaxed and enjoy the holidays like never before. Christmas was about peace and joy, and family togetherness, and scrumptious food. She wanted him to experience it all the max. The welcoming feast had gone remarkably well.

The main house was made of concrete and would withstand the highest level typhoons, but it was small and wouldn't accommodate the entire family. So Erica and her cousins went about building grass shack additions that would be comfortable and cool for the visiting couples, and would allow them some privacy. She planned all the doorways around the outside kitchen, so that everyone could gather at the kitchen tables. The structures wouldn't withstand heavy winds but there were no forecasts about any massive storms coming up Typhoon Alley across the Pacific. The last major storms had veered around Yap and Guam but had wreaked havoc on the Philippines. Hundreds of people had died in the flooding and strong winds, and then later on in major mud slides.

Constantine, Belle and Andre arrived two days later. They had brought along Leilani, one of Erica's favorite second cousins by marriage. She would be a great source of ideas and information, being a personnel director for a large insurance firm on Guam. All four of them were loaded down with Christmas gifts bought at the US Navy Base and colorfully wrapped. As in the past, Erica knew it would be fun and functional presents, items that couldn't be bought in Yap at any of the stores. Papa John was sitting under his favorite banyan tree, surrounded by red hibiscus flowers. He had a huge smile.

Constantine and Belle's daughter came bounding out the jungle, accompanied by her cousin Andrew, Eduardo's son. More hugs went around. Sweetie had grown to a gorgeous young lady and was doing well on Yap. Constantine said once they got settled in Guam, that they wanted to bring her up to stay and finish high school and to prepare for college.

After everyone had greeted each other and hugged again, Erica pulled Constantine and Belle to the side, and said that she had to talk to them later about her career and travel plans. Constantine responded, "Baby Sister, it's about time. We all wondered if you were going to rot away on this little island. You're bright and got it together, and you should be out there in the big world, enjoying and experimenting what to do with your life."

Erica said, "Now you sound like Mom."

Belle added, "Erica, Constantine and your mom are right on. You have so much to offer. We'll help you anyway we can. We always have an extra bedroom at our house, and it's close to the University of Guam. You could start next year." Everyone was careful to skirt around the fact that John might be dying in a few months and everything was basically on hold until the following year. It was obvious that Erica could start her own life afterwards, and maybe her mother might want to move. When she mentioned the moving to Constantine, he felt that it would be unlikely that their mother would leave Ulithi, wanting to be close to John's grave, and also raising the grandchildren. He also knew that Anna did much of her art business through email and the US Post Office, so the move wouldn't be necessary for her livelihood.

Helen and Ronnie arrived the next day with their baby. It was obvious that Helen was pregnant but not so far along that she worried about flying or not being able to find medical services if needed.

The additional rooms were finished quickly, just needing some bamboo poles and palm thatch for the roof and walls, and the families moved in, getting comfortable and organized. Andre elected to sleep in the big front room in the main house with Sweetie and Andrew, and other family members and assorted neighbors. Sleeping arrangements were informal in the islands, and it wasn't unusual for people to sleep in different houses. Parents didn't worry when their children not coming home because often they just stayed with their friends, and crimes against children and females were unheard of in this peaceful island environment.

Constantine and Andre slipped into their thus. The way the thu fit, Andre's backside wound was quite obvious. He would have one large scar. Ronnie decided not go native all the way because as he said, "I would just look goofy and very white in a thu. Might even get a bad sunburn on my butt."

Belle and Leilani jumped into their lava-lavas, but decided to wear a top garment, not out of modesty because, as Belle laughingly said, "Gravity has taken its toll." Anna came out wearing only her lava-lava and said, "All part of life, Girls. Not to worry. These breasts made my children healthy and strong." Of course, Erica was perfect, careful never to get sunburned and never had babies.

Chapter 12

ANDREW AND SWEETIE

When Eduardo had left Yap for Guam and the mainland in his young doper days, he left behind the cutest little boy named Andrew. He was the result of a quick, irresponsible romance, not only by Eduardo but also his jungle, equally immature girlfriend, Lorena. They had both got crazy on alcohol and marijuana, ran off into the jungle, she raised her lava-lava, and they made hot, torrid love in the pouring rain, twice in fact. It was a crazy love scene right out of a dramatic movie, complete with a muddy taro patch, but ready for a commitment or settling down. Eduardo had a drug problem and Lorena, she just liked to party and ended up going off with a visiting "carnie" who took her as far as Saipan, and then dumped her when he found out she was with child. She prostituted herself three times to get enough money for an airplane ticket back home.

She was befriended by a local policeman who found her wandering along the beach in the darkness after one of her "service calls" in a tourist's rental car. The policeman took her for coffee, showered her up and bought her some vitamins and nutritional food for her and the new baby's health. They parted on good terms and each promised to stay in touch.

She came back to Yap and had the baby, and fortunately the alcohol and drugs had not turned the boy, little Andrew into a FAS victim. The girl's family had disowned her, so she flew up to Guam to be with her policeman friend. She had two more babies in quick succession, grew tired of the family life, and did some more prostitution and raised enough money to fly off to the mainland. No one had heard of her since, including the policemen and her two children that she left on Saipan.

With Eduardo and his girlfriend both gone, Anna and John ended up with a special new baby boy. He was a lovable little guy and everyone took to him after he captivated them with his big smile. While growing up, Andrew never had time to worry about his parentage or "his place in the sun." He just knew he was loved by many people. Erica became his surrogate mother, and he learned how to snorkel and fish by following Papa throughout the day. He did well in school and was athletic and won several swim contests in his age group. He was the favorite of the family, until another grandchild, Sweetie, came along, about a year younger than Andrew. He found himself sharing the main family attention with this newcomer.

Sweetie was the youngest child of Constantine and Belle, Andre's little sister. Her real name was Grace, but she was so nice and sweet, that her nickname became Sweetie, and it stuck. Constantine was off in the Army most of the time, and Belle wanted to establish a career for herself in marriage and family counseling. During a visit to Guam, Anna saw the schedule that Belle was trying to maintain with her college classes, and getting Sweetie to pre-school and for baby shots. Her grades were suffering. Anna talked it over with John, and before long, Sweetie was on the way to Ulithi with Grandma Anna to start her island life. She loved her Grandma and Papa John, and she adjusted quickly.

Andrew wasn't thrilled by this interloper into his grandparent domain; there was little tension and jealousy in the beginning. But before long, Sweetie won him over with her sharing and a willingness to compromise, and Andrew was certain to win her over. All he had to do was give her one of his thousand watt smiles. The two bonded over the next six months and went to school together, happily walking and forth every day to their schoolhouse that housed six grades in two rooms. The grandparents never had to worry about traffic or kid-nappings by perverts or deranged "wanna-bee" parents, and this safe environment made Belle and Constantine secure and content. Belle knew that she would be bringing Sweetie back into their Guam home as soon as she completed her classes. Belle was so thankful to Anna, and soon her high GPA maxed out. She missed the little girl every day and managed to get her on the phone twice a week. Grandma Anna sent lots of photos.

Andrew was another matter in the relative area, and thank good-ness he adjusted so quickly to his relatives. His mother never cor-responded and contact with Eduardo had been minimal, which was probably best since the family knew a child shouldn't be raised by a dope addict. The recent news was promising in that Eduardo might be cleaning up his act and coming home. Ronnie and Helen were optimistic about his recovery.

Time would tell the story about the two youngsters. Sweetie's fu-ture was pretty much destined for success and education. Andrew's future had a lot of variables involving Eduardo's condition but the main ingredient in the mix that he could expect was love and support from the rest of Sapelaluts. The best part of that formula was that he knew it and was content and comfortable in his life. He liked who he was and wouldn't be needing a shrink, or drugs, in his future.

Andrew had heard the conversation that his biological father, Eduardo, was coming to Ulithi. He seemed to take the news in stride.

Anna said, "It's going to be fine with your father. If it doesn't work out, we'll still be here to take care of you."

"Auntie Erica says that he gives her the heebie-jeebies. What's that mean?"

"That means he gives her the willies, makes her nervous and jumpy. She just doesn't know him very well, and it's no secret; he has been using drugs and got in trouble with the police. He left when Auntie Erica was a young teenager."

"I hope he's nice."

Sweetie said, "Of course, he's nice. He's my Papa's brother, and Papa wouldn't bring him here if he wasn't nice. My Papa and your Papa will be bringing us presents for Christmas. I just know it."

"I hope you're right about everything."

"It'll be fine. Trust me." Anna patted him on the back and fixed him some toast for breakfast with fresh mango jam. She knew how to make a young boy happy.

Andrew looked out to sea in the direction of Yap Proper. Sweetie said, "He'll be here soon. Hey, you wanna go swimming near the old crashed Japanese zero?"

"Right after my toast. That plane is a good place to snorkel. I like all the orange and shiny fish that swim around the wreck."

Chapter 13

TROUBLE IN GUAM

Eduardo had a few bad days at the shelter. During his withdrawal from drugs and alcohol, his brain was bouncing around in his skull, at least it seemed that way to him and that's what he told the medical workers. He got into argument with one the nurses at the shelter about more recovery drugs; actually what he wanted was handful of pain pills, which would put him on his downhill spiral. The nurse told him flat out that if he didn't cooperate and calm down, he was back on the streets. He continued to verbally harass her until she motioned at a security officer. Eduardo relaxed before the guard could intervene.

After the guard walked away, Eduardo was back at the nurse's station, verbally berating her insensitivity and told her that she "was stupid." When she turned to use the phone to call 911, Eduardo took her by the shoulder trying to intimidate her. He yelled, "I'm not going to hurt you. I just need something to stop my pain. My head is bursting."

The guard immediately responded and took hold of Eduardo and pulled him away from the nurse. At the same time, the shelter doctor, Dr. Carey, arrived and ordered Eduardo to calm down. The nurse asked, "Should I call 911?"

Dr. Carey said, "No, it's okay. I've got him now." He thanked the nurse and the security officer, and told Eduardo to apologize. He did and bowed his head and asked forgiveness.

Dr. Carey walked him to his office. Eduardo talked and talked, releasing all his frustration and anxiety. The doctor told him in no uncertain terms that was the last time that he would ever lay hands on anyone on the staff or a fellow resident. The doctor assured him that the police would be called next time and that he was out of the program, and on his own. He explained that this was his chance to recover and get back on track, and judging by his poor health, there weren't a lot of chances left.

Dr. Carey said firmly, "There are a hundred other people that want to get a chance at recovery. Right now, the government is picking up the bill and figuring you are worth the risk. If I say 'go-away,' and you are argumentative and belligerent, or lay hands on anyone, you will be busted for assault and be out!"

"I understand. I will cooperate. I wanna get back to Yap and see my family. My father is dying from heart disease. I wanna see him before he passes on. And I wanna see my son, Andrew. My sister Helen tells me he is strong and good athlete."

"I know all that. I read your chart, and have talked to your brother and sister. So it's up to you. I can't do it for you."

Eduardo had hit bottom and he knew it. He had to get back up and enjoy his family and live a sane life again. He cooperated fully for the next two weeks, and now it was past Thanksgiving Day, and the days were flying off the calendar until he headed to Yap for Christmas. He was waiting for the okay from Dr. Carey. He asked every day. Meanwhile his headaches had abated and he had been eating properly and doing aerobic exercises on the treadmill. No smoking or betel nut. He gained twelve pounds and had become friends with the nurse and the nutritionist.

On December 1, he asked again if he could leave. Much to his surprise, Dr. Carey gave his approval. He then went through several hours of counseling of what to expect on the outside and what the old temptations would be like. He knew that he mustn't associate with his old street pals or he would be right back addicted. It was arranged through the nurse that he would take the next flight to Guam the following day. Constantine had left an E- ticket for him as planned with Helen and Ronnie.

Dr. Carey drove him to the airport the next day, chitchatting about his recovery and what his plans were. It was a regular, coherent conversation, which he had missed during his trip to drugged-out hell. He couldn't remember having a normal discussion with someone in over five years. Dr. Carey parked the car and got him through the departure counters and left him waving goodbye at the security checkpoint. Eduardo walked proudly and briskly and actually felt healthy, which was another condition he hadn't experienced in years.

The Continental flight was on time and he soon found himself winging across the Pacific to Hawaii and then on to Guam. It was a long arduous trip but he amused himself with pleasant thoughts and the fantastic music system in the armrest. Constantine had renewed his Micronesian passport so he didn't expect problems at the Guam Immigration counter.

But his outlaw past was about to catch up with him. Karma always kept track.

Something significant apparently popped up on the immigration computer at the border point, and he was escorted to a private interview room by two US Customs and Immigration Officers. There were three arrest warrants for him in the computer, one for petty theft, one for not paying traffic fines, but the one that got the attention of the federal officers was for the sale of drugs. Smuggling of drugs in and out of Guam is a major problem and a felony with a long prison term.

Eduardo and his luggage were searched thoroughly with negative results. The narcotics dog had no interest in his bags. A medical technician was called and an intrusive search was conducted in all the orifices of his body. All searches were negative. An interview also proved negative. Eduardo explained that he was just left detox and that he was on his way to see his ailing father on Yap.

Seeing no US violations, the federal officers released him to the Guam Police as follow-up on the arrest warrants. Taking Dr. Carey's advice, he remained calm and cool each step of the way. He was booked routinely into the Department of Corrections and given his two phone calls, one to an attorney and the other to a family member. He was basically broke and knew that an attorney wouldn't discuss his case unless he had up some up-front money or the court appointed a lawyer for him.

He called Constantine and miraculously his collect call went through the first time, and Constantine was at the house. Eduardo explained his predicament, and when Constantine asked him about drugs, he answered, "No way, Man. I'm off that stuff. I'm clean."

"Mind if I talk to a Corrections Officer?"

"Not at all. Let me ask one to come to the phone."

Officer Felix Navarro answered the phone. Constantine introduced himself, and as luck would have it, Officer Navarro was in the Army Reserve and had completed a tour in Iraq. It appeared that at one time, their tours overlapped, and they were only three miles apart for almost two months. Constantine said, "Hard to tell whose who. We kinda all look alike in that camo uniform and of course, covered with sand."

"You got that right. That's the first time I've ever had sunglasses sand-blasted by the wind. What can I do for you?"

"Probably by now, you know Eduardo is my brother. He's been down a crooked path but he's on the way back to living the good life. He just finished detox on the mainland." He paused and asked, "Was he clean and okay with you guys and the feds?"

"Yep, he's been cooperative with everyone. He wasn't carrying dope, no dope tracks on his body, and our dog wasn't interested in him or his luggage."

"This is the favor I need, especially for my parents who are worried sick. Please do a breathalyzer, and then have him pee in a cup for dope testing."

CHRISTMAS IN THE TROPICS

"We can do the breathalyzer right now, but he doesn't smell like booze. Also he displays no sign of intoxication. He's coherent and not acting stupid."

"Can you do the cup thing?"

"Sure, if he agrees. We can't analyze it until morning, but I don't think we'll find anything."

"*Kammagar*, please do it anyway. If he's scientifically clean, than our parents will feel better, and so will his rehab doctor."

"Consider it done. I'll put Eduardo back on the phone. He'll be going to court tomorrow on the afternoon calendar, probably about 1330 hours. If you get up here, you can get rid of the traffic charge just by paying $315 to the court clerk. At least you'll have the charges down to two."

Eduardo took the phone back. Constantine explained what was going to happen. He added that they would have a family meeting. Then if everyone was in agreement, then he and Ronnie would catch a boat to Yap Proper and then fly up to Guam. It would take two days to make all the connections. Meanwhile, Constantine told him to sit tight, be cooperative and take the urine test. He told him he wouldn't be making a guilty or innocence plea in court yet, as the first step would be arraignment and setting the bail. He added that most charges have a set bail, none of his charges being extremely high. Since he was indigent, the court would also appoint a lawyer on the felony dope charge.

Eduardo asked, "What will I do for bail money? I'm flat broke. I think I have about $10 to my name. I might have to do some jail time."

"That's what the family meeting will be about. Should we take a chance on you staying straight? If everyone is in agreement, then Andre and I both have hazard pay from Iraq. I know my son would be willing to help out."

"You guys are so great. I think Ronnie will be supportive. He's been on my side since I decided to dry out. He got me referred to rehab."

"Yeah, Ronnie sitting next to me on the extension. He just keeps nodding approval."

"If the family gets me out of here, this will be the best Christmas present ever. Have our father relax, so his condition doesn't get worse. I need to do a lot of explaining to that old man."

Ronnie said, "Keep the faith. Good things are going to happen. We'll be out fishing on the big wide Pacific before you know it."

"I believe you guys. You taught me a valuable lesson about family and what really counts in life."

"Just stay strong and focused. You're in a controlled environment right now. It might be a little different when you walk through a marijuana plantation on one of the outer islands."

"Not to worry. I wanna get back to a regular life and my computer work. I've got some great new ideas for software."

Chapter 14

THE FAMILY AT CHRISTMAS

Fairly confident that the family would approve of their intervention with Eduardo and knowing the number of seats was limited on the planes, Constantine quickly put all the plans in motion before the family meeting. He arranged for a float plane to come to Ulithi and take him and Ronnie to Yap Proper to the International Airport. Ronnie booked their flight on Continental Airlines to Guam. Constantine spoke to Andre who agreed to a loan to Eduardo for whatever was needed. He reminded Constantine that he had wedding plans with Vicky. As expected because of the connections, they wouldn't be able to get to Guam for two days.

Constantine talked to Mother Anna before the family meeting. She said that Papa John had had a good sleep and that he was able to handle the news about Eduardo. The family group had dinner and then took seats around a large picnic table and watched the sun set into the Pacific. There was a slight, cooling breeze. Erica brought out a homemade coconut drink *tuba* that some of the adult family members enjoyed like an after dinner liqueur.

Constantine explained the situation. Ronnie, Helen, Andre and he had all talked about Eduardo with his doctor and counselors, and the shelter workers, and it was a consensus opinion that Eduardo was determined to stay sober. Constantine told them about the arrest on Guam for his previous crimes and that he wasn't denying any of it, or making excuses that they were all trumped-up charges. He was also clean regarding drugs and alcohol. All the searches at the airport and the jail showed that he wasn't carrying drugs, and hadn't even had the free alcoholic drinks on the plane. Officer Navarro had called and Eduardo's breathalyzer and urine tests had come back negative.

Papa John asked, "This is an expensive rescue call. Who's going to pay for the plane tickets, and then his bail and fines at the jail? Mother and I can help but when you're retired, you're on a fixed income. There's no extra money coming in."

"Andre and I both have bonus money from Iraq. I talked it over with Belle, and André called his fiancée Vicky in Germany. The ladies are supportive of us spending the money. We all agreed that Eduardo can make it back to sobriety. He knows that this is his last big chance. If he blows it, we lose money, but if relapses, he knows he'll be dead before he ever sees fifty years old. He's got a lot more at stake."

The family voted one hundred percent to help Eduardo. Constantine called Officer Navarro and asked him to let Eduardo know that everything was in motion, and that he should be patient and go through the court process. He added, Constantine with his sense of humor and knowing that Eduardo would get a laugh, "Tell him 'relax and be happy.' That's one of our favorite sayings on Yap. We use it whenever it's getting crazy in politics or when the weather is crappy and not good for going out on a boat."

Officer Navarro replied, "Yep, same on Guam. He's doing okay. He's already made some new friends."

Constantine said, "That could be bad. Hope they're not dopers."

"No, they're some petty theft guys, stealing copper. With the economy down, a lot of the unemployed youngsters are stealing what they can, especially to the Chinese who want anything that can be recycled. I'll fix my eyes on Eduardo and keep you posted. Right now, he's doing fine."

"Thanks again. I'll see you in a few days. Maybe we'll enjoy a cool one together after you're off work."

"It's a deal. Soldier to soldier."

Christmas in the Tropics

Eduardo went to court and was informed of his charges. His total bail was set at five thousand dollars. A family member could pay ten percent of that and guarantee the rest with land or a bank account. Eduardo was remanded back to jail.

Two days later, Constantine and Ronnie arrived. Constantine paid off the traffic charge in the court, and now Eduardo was facing only two charges. His passport had been seized by the court and he wasn't allowed to leave the island. Through his court-appointed lawyer, Tony Pickens, he asked for a bail modification and permission to leave the island to be home for Christmas. Constantine and Ronnie appeared in court with him for the hearing.

Constantine asked to address the court. It was allowed by the district court judge. He told the judge about Eduardo's rehab and that he was drug-free, that their father was dying and wanted all his children home for Christmas, and that he and Ronnie, a brother-in-law, would guarantee that Eduardo would appear for all court hearings. He also asserted that Eduardo wanted to plead guilty to the theft charge and get it off the scheduled hearings. The judge looked at Attorney Pickens, who nodded his approval.

The judge indicated that he would take a thirty-minute recess and review the file on Eduardo. The petty theft case involved Eduardo being drunk and walking out of a Mom-and-Pop store without paying for a case of beer. There was no violence involved. When the Chinese shop owner stopped Eduardo in the parking lot, Eduardo made up some lame excuse that he forgot to pay but he didn't try to run. The police arrived and upon seeing that Eduardo had no money, arrested him for petty theft. He was released the next day because of jail overcrowding.

The judge returned to the court room and promptly addressed Eduardo and asked Constantine to step forward. "I see your traffic fine has been paid. That charge is off the docket. Regarding the petty theft and you pleading guilty, your guilty plea is accepted and you are sentenced to jail for one day, but I will give "time served" credit for your jail booking time. You are to write a letter of apology to the shop owner. You are also fined one hundred dollars and assessed court costs of two hundred and twenty-five dollars. Can you pay?"

Constantine said, "Yes, Your Honor. We can pay that one."

The judge continued, "Pay a total of $325 and that charge is adjudicated. Now on the narcotics sales charge. I see you were allegedly selling marijuana; it appears to be about one-half pound to a police informant. I want you to discuss this one with your attorney, as it could result in prison time. We will set that hearing about January 15."

The lawyer asked, "How about the bail reduction and him leaving for Yap?"

"I will reduce the bail to four thousand dollars, with ten percent required in cash. I see that Constantine Sapelalut is a soldier on leave from Iraq, also in the islands to see his ailing father. I will accept four hundred dollars in cash, and a signed promissory note that basically says if Eduardo does not show up as required, that Constantine will have to pay the court thirty-six hundred dollars. Is that agreeable to you, Constantine?"

"Yes, Your Honor. Can you release his passport?"

He glanced at his court clerk, and said, "Release the passport to the defendant. Once the ten percent is paid, the defendant is free to go."

Constantine stated, "Judge, thank you so much. Our parents will appreciate Eduardo coming home after being gone for over six years."

The judge smiled and said, "It's Christmas time. Time for cheer and happy tidings, and good will to all men." He looked directly at Eduardo and said, "Eduardo, don't let me down, and especially your family. Be true to them and yourself."

Close to tears, Eduardo said, "Thank you, Your Honor. I won't let anyone down. I promise you that!"

Chapter 15

HISTORY AND MEMORIES

Like other patients with his heart problems, John had begun thinking about his past and his early life. But since he had received the death sentence from his doctor, he thought more deeply about mortality and what lie ahead, could it be heaven or hell, or maybe a fall into a dark abyss with no bottom and no escaping. Possibly he would just return to dust as the Bible said.

But he was still extremely interested about who came before him – his ancestors and the previous cultures.

On a coupla days, he just sat on the beach and stared at the horizon. At the end of the day, he would be depressed and felt that he had just wasted another precious day. He would have to take a pill to sleep.

One day a part of his brain clicked on an idea, somewhat constructive to do with his remaining days, rather than moping. He decided to record the past so his children would better understand their lives and culture, and could prepare for what lie ahead. He had passed much of his known verbal history to his children, but he was also an academic and had assembled a number of books and articles about the islands in the past and where the original peoples had come from, and how life was under the different colonial powers. The earliest arrivals in Micronesia left very little information and artifacts that had withstood centuries of humid tropical weather. Just about everything in the islands either rots or rusts away.

Through the best guesses of archaeologists, anthropologists, and historians, it is believed that the Austronesian-speaking peoples entered the Pacific Regions from Southeast Asia more than three thousand years ago. Their first stops were probably the Marianas Islands, and then into the Western Carolines; from there settling in the Eastern Caroline Islands (Pohnpei, Chuuk, etc.) and into the Marshall Islands. Found beads on Yap and weaving looms still used in the Micronesia Islands which are of Indonesian design, have been uncovered. Even though there are a dozen or more different languages throughout Micronesia, there are some similar words and sounds. These are clues to the past. The early societies were apparently matriarchal with land owned and passed on to wives and children, but was later changed with the male-dominated societies with chiefs and clans on Yap, Palau and other parts of Micronesia.

John kept flipping through his books and jotting down notes, being sure to summarize the history of the islands for his children and grandchildren. Yap was well-known for its great sea voyagers, and Yap was a regular trading center as the Micronesians kept in touch with each other, and probably Asia; and also there were significant civilizations in the past as shown by the magnificent ruins (Nan Madol) of Pohnpei and Kosrae, the stone money of Yap, the *latte* foundations of Guam, Rota and Tinian, and the basalt monoliths and terraces of Babeldaob.

Explorer Ferdinand Magellan was the first to sail on the Pacific in an expedition financed by the king Spain in an effort in 1519. He set off with five ships and lost two vessels in storms at the tip of South America. The three remaining ships sailed northwest for eleven days and came upon people in swift outrigger canoes on Guam. The local people, Chamorros, stole one of his skiffs and in vengeance Magellan took forty armed men ashore and burned fifty houses, killed seven men and recovered his boat. From there he sailed to Indonesia and then onto Mactan Island in the Philippines ,where he was trying to subdue and convert the local inhabitants to Christianity Chief Lapu-

Lapu took offense and killed Magellan and twenty of his men. One of his ships managed to circumnavigate the globe, going alone across the Indian Ocean, around the Cape of Good Hope, and north through the Atlantic, reaching Seville, Spain in 1522. One hundred and seventy men of the Spanish crews died on the voyage.

No one else bothered with going around the globe until Sir Francis Drake of England did so in 1578. The predominant route for the Spanish was indirect to Mexico and Central America, across land to the Pacific and then travel by its Pacific Fleet to Manila. Micronesia was still ignored, until 1668, when Spain used Guam as a support base for their galleons going across the Pacific with silver, tea, silk, and spices loaded on from the Philippines, China and other Asian ports.

Little attention was paid to the rest of Micronesia until 1864 when the first resident German trader set up a trading store in the Marshalls, followed in 1869 with a post on Yap. Germany established a protectorate over the Marshalls and then attempted to extend this to all of the Caroline Island in 1885. The Spanish objected saying that they had claimed the area in earlier explorations, and in 1874, the Pope mediated the Spanish-German dispute and ruled in favor of the Spanish on most issues, but gave the Marshall Islands to Germany for trading and annexation.

In the 1830's whalers came from Australia, followed by the Americans in the 1850's. These newcomers brought catastrophic epidemics and foreign control over the surviving local peoples and much of the traditional way of island life was eliminated. The protestant missionaries came and established themselves on Pohnpei and Kosrae by 1852, and nothing was ever the same again. John chuckled to himself. "And they brought Christmas and other religious holidays." John enjoyed Christmas and Easter and thought some of the changes were for the best, plus all the medical advances that allowed people to survive not only the European diseases but also diseases common to the tropics with particular bacteria strains and parasites.

In 1898 the Spanish-American War busted up Spain's colonial empire, and the US annexed Guam and the Philippines as US possessions. The Spanish sold the Carolines and the northern Marians

to the Germans in 1899. The Germans went right to work and organized a lucrative copra trade and a poll tax. If the locals couldn't
pay, they were put to work on the road as slave labor. The Ponapeians
revolted, killed the German governor but soon the rebel leaders were
rounded up and executed and dumped in a mass grave.

When World War I broke out, Germany basically abandoned its
Pacific possessions; and by agreement with the British, the Japanese
took over the Northern Marianas, the Carolines and the Marshalls
without a fight. After the War, Japan was appointed to administer
the former German colonies under a League of Nations mandate. In
1935, Japan withdrew from the League of Nations and began building large military installations all over *Nanyo Gunto* (Japan's name for
Micronesia). The Japanese South Seas Government *Nanyochokan* was
based in Koror, Palau.

Laying down a book, John called out for Anna and said that he
needed a rest, and that he would start up again in doing the outline
of Micronesian history. He figured it was a good time to research
and write while Constantine and Ronnie were in Saipan trying to get
Eduardo out of jail. Anna put him in bed for two hours and then
woke him for dinner. Afterwards he went back to his research and
outlining. His pen couldn't keep up with his fast-flowing, energetic
mind.

Japan encouraged emigration to Micronesia and by 1940 there
were 84,476 Japanese residing in Micronesia, which equaled a full
two-thirds of the entire population. The island society that followed
had three classes of people: Japanese at the top; Korean and Okinawan
workers in the middle and Micronesians (*toming*) at the bottom. The
local people continued to live by subsistence agriculture and making
copra, while Japan controlled all of the economic and educational activities in the region. Interisland travel by canoe was banned and the
authority of the traditional chiefs undermined.

Japan hoped to extend it imperialist power throughout the entire Pacific Region. Their military hoped to disable the Americans
by attacking Pearl Harbor in 1941. This attack only mobilized the
Americans and cemented their resolve to defeat the Germans and

CHRISTMAS IN THE TROPICS

Japanese in World War II on two fronts. After the decisive victories by the Americans in Palau, Truk Lagoon, Saipan, Guam, and Iwo Jima, and the atomic bombing of Hiroshima and Nagasaki, the Japanese surrendered unconditionally. The Micronesian islands were placed under the administration of the United States by the United Nations through the auspices of the Trust Territory of the Pacific Islands.

Since 1945, the Micronesian peoples have organized themselves into three government political entities through the Compacts of Free Association with the United States: Palau, the Marshall Islands, and the Federated States of Micronesia (Kosrae, Pohnpei, Chuuk and Yap). The name Micronesia means "Little Islands" with a total land-mass equal to that of Rhode Island or the Los Angeles Basin with about one-half million people. Only 125 islands are inhabited. John always smiled when people asked where his tiny island was, and he would reply, "Think of the distance between San Francisco and New York City on a map, and it's probably close to Denver, way out the Pacific surrounded by water and more water. It's just a little dot on the globe." The people of Micronesia can come and go into the United States, work there or join the military, and reap all the benefits of any American such as health, education, welfare, housing and so on. The people of Guam and the Commonwealth of the Northern Marianas Islands are full US citizens.

John attributed much of his own education, and his training and job opportunities directly related to Micronesia's association with the United States. Many of his students had gone on to successful careers on the mainland. Two of his students were high-ranking officers in the Army.

Anna took a phone call. It was Constantine with the latest news about Eduardo. Anna said, "Good news, my Sweet man. Two charges have been taken care of for Eduardo, and now he's looking at only the drug selling charge."

"Does that mean he'll be home for Christmas?"

"We'll know for sure tomorrow. The two boys are working on getting bail posted and his passport returned. We'll know tomorrow. They might release him to Constantine."

"Good, it sounds like he wants to get clean and get on with his life. He needs a good woman like his mother to keep things on track. The way things are going, he might even be back in time for Constantine and Andre's birthdays. It's shaping up to be good year."

Anna bowed her head and started to cry. She whispered, "Not in every way."

"My Darling Girl, we've had a good run. Think how wonderful our life has been…and besides I'm not dead yet. In fact, I really feel great after my nap."

She answered, "You look strong. Your color is good."

"You're darned right I'm strong. Let's take a walk on our beach. It's a full moon, and that big white ball always makes me wanna do wild and crazy things."

They kissed, and Anna pulled him to her feet and off they went to their beach, both bare-chested, wearing only garments over their midsections.

She stated, "Isn't it just too wonderful to be free!"

"I'm always free when I'm with you."

Grandchild Sweetie, sitting at water's edge said to her friend, "My Grandpa and my Grandma forgot their flip-flops. I hope they don't step on a sharp shell."

The friend replied, "You don't have to worry. All grandparents have real tough feet. They've been walking a long time."

"Yeah, you're right, and they're real careful where they step."

"That's for sure."

Chapter 16

COFFEE KLATSCH, YAPESE STYLE

After the beach stroll and getting John showered and tucked into bed, Anna went to the outside kitchen and found the adult females of her family in a lively discussion. They were talking about men and romance, and the woman's role in Yapese society. She wasn't sure that she wanted to hear what her daughter-in-law Belle might say about her son Constantine. It was raw but positive, and led her to believe that there was still a lot of burning embers in their relationship.

Belle asserted, "Oops, Mother Anna is here. I better not be too explicit."

Anna said, "Go ahead. I've been a married woman for a long time. You must keep your man happy in the bedroom and vice-versa, or problems start, like the roving eye. As far as I know, my man had always stayed in his own yard."

Belle added, "That's what I've been saying. Constantine has been faithful and loyal, and he's been a very active boy since he's been home. He's horny every night."

Erica laughed, "What else could he be, for goodness sake. He's been in a Muslim country. If he strays and has a relationship with a local girl, the family could murder her just to keep their so-called honor, and he would be responsible. That would be enough responsibility to take the starch out of any guy's interest."

"That's true, but Constantine could have strayed with a female US or British soldier, or a civilian clerk, or some other woman when he's in transit, or on special assignment. He was in England for six months."

Belle's sister Leilani said, "How would you ever know if the guy's discreet? My husband was dogging for a year before I knew it.'

Belle replied, "A woman knows, especially a wife when you're with a man 24/7. You had hints about your husband before the truth came out. Remember those strange e-mails and then phone calls."

"Yeah, you're probably right. I know he lost interest in me. I didn't wanna face up to it…have a confrontation. I didn't want the hurt or ugliness. But don't you think all men are dogs?"

Anna said, "Men are visual oriented, but I think most husbands have to sneak a glance occasionally, maybe even fantasize, but most have the good sense to not make a move. They have so much to lose, and in the long run, all they have is the wife or lover, and good health. We both know that for sure. We've had some real insightful conversations. I know he's thought about it. You know how it works in the island jungles – so fast and secretive. Just a wink, or a gesture with the eyebrows. Up comes the lava-lava. It's that fast. Several of his students, long past school and married, have invited him into the jungle. He's had the good sense to turn them away, and he told me about it. One of the girls had contracted a STD on the mainland and gave a dose to one of our politicians."

Erica laughed and said, "How come I never get invited into the jungle?"

One of her cousins, Joanna, said, "Maybe you should do the inviting."

Belle exclaimed, "And quit riding those coconuts. We saw you out there yesterday." The women all knew that "riding the coconut" was a form of natural masturbation, where the woman places a coconut up between her legs and rides the incoming waves.

Erica pointed at the group and said, "Hey, I've seen you girls in the waves before!"

CHRISTMAS IN THE TROPICS

Everyone laughed out loud. They were teasing her, knowing she was still a virgin. If a dark brown person could get red with embarrassment, she did.

Joanna was on a roll and exclaimed, "Erica, you need to get that chastity belt unlocked. You're probably getting all rusty by now. Find the key. We won't tell the padre if you don't."

Erica flushed again and said, "You girls stop it, you hear."

Helen said, "You know the old saying, 'Try it, you might like it!' Truer words were never said. Then if you decided you liked it and only had a jungle quickie, you would be walking around wondering what the hell happened. Jungle mating is too fast. I think you should go away to college for a career and find a real love mate, somebody you can enjoy being with, like going to the movies or just bundling up in the cold, and the other physical things just fall into place."

Leilani added, "A career is good but you can't snuggle up to it at night. The love mate is the best part. Just go slow and find the right person."

Erica said, "I've have already talked about it with Mother and Papa. Next year I go to college, just as soon as things are under control here."

Joanna added, "You go whenever you can. I can help out here. My husband will be finished with college in five months, and I will either join him or he'll come back here. You need to get off this rock."

Anna asked, "Do I notice a little bump on your tummy. Did hubby Henry leave you a little souvenir?"

"Yeah, you noticed right. That Henry boy has a good aim and strong seed…but then again, it took him about thirty-one times to get it right but who's counting? We kept track by putting a marble in a jar every time we did it."

Erica said, "Thirty-one times, I can't imagine. You females are going to drive me crazy with all this men talk. I hope I won't turn into a little hussy when I get to college."

Belle smiled, "Not to worry. You parents brought you up right, and you go to church, and you know what's right, what's wrong. Another old saying is, 'If it doesn't feel right, then it's wrong.' You know what's appropriate down deep in your innards."

Leilani asked, "Do you girls wanna watch some movies? I brought them down from Guam – some very nice love stories with happy endings."

Erica asked, "Are you trying to make my love life look worse?"

Leilani said, "Look, I've been separated from my dog husband for six months. I haven't been dating, just hanging out with my friends and staying busy. I work a little overtime at work. I volunteer for the Red Cross and do some local theater work. You can do the same. When the right guy comes along, it'll just happen, but your selection possibilities in the middle of the Pacific Ocean are limited big-time."

Erica couldn't let it go and said, "Maybe you should ride the coconuts with me."

Leilani chuckled, "I am about ready for sure."

Helen said, "I can show you girls some new embroidery patterns or we could go through some catalogs and get some ideas what to order through the mail. I could also send back some of your choices from the mainland when Ronnie and I get back. Also picked up some good *lechon* recipes off the internet."

Belle replied, "Hmmm…maybe tomorrow. How about we discuss how Yapese women are faring in the modern times, dealing with the old traditions and how women should be seen but not heard in public meetings."

Anna answered, "Not much changed there. But it has never been bad for most of the women. Sometimes women don't want to be involved in whether a sewer is overflowing into some neighbor's taro field, or if some farmer is taking more than his share from the public coconut trees. The men can talk about fishing lures and style of fishing for hours and hours, and where to go during what season. Let the men make those decisions."

"But how are you treated at home? Who makes all the decisions?"

Anna laughed and said, "Listen and listen good. You experienced ladies already know. Women throughout the world basically run the household and raise the children. If the man is half-way smart, and he likes his dinner on time, and his clothes washed, and a little sugar at night, then he has to treat his woman with dignity and respect. Even if the man is a polygamist, generally if he upsets one wife, then the other wives will not be happy either. It must be hell if all his wives are pissed off at the same time. The Muslim men act and talk tough, but they had better be nice to their wives or their lives will also be miserable. Can you imagine having four mother-in-laws and maybe a coupla matchmakers all angry at you at the same time?"

Helen added, "Or having four father-in-laws banging on your door, along with a passel of brothers?"

Belle said, "Well said. My Muslim lady friend, Beya, from Davao in the Philippines is a second wife. Her husband plays the bigshot in public but when he's home, he's nice to all four wives and the children are mutually cared for by one and all. My friend is able to socialize and shop with me, but cannot be around other males unless her husband or brother is around. She seems to be happy. That's how she was raised and doesn't know any difference. She would never consider divorce unless the husband beat her or mistreated in some other way. She might eyeball other guys but never talks about it. She dresses very plain, but her undergarments are hot and sexy."

Leilani laughed, "So the Muslim chicks like to be hot too!"

Belle added, "That's true. She's still a woman, right?"

Joanna asked, "What's next on our plans? What do you girls wanna do?"

Anna suggested, "What if we play some board games and open a few bottles of wine. That should be fun."

Erica chuckled, "I'm ready for a few giggles. I might even get a little drunk. I'm so glad that Papa thinks I should go to the mainland."

"Not too much drinking, Missy," said Anna.

"Mama, you know me. I sniff the wineglass and I'm already giddy."

Leilani asserted, "Bring on the games. Open that wine! I'm feeling like a winner tonight."

Belle said to Erica, "No more of that 'running off into the jungle' talk.' You gotta be a good girl, no naughtiness for you, or Santa will paddle right past your grass shack."

Leilani couldn't let that straight-line fade away and said, "Or paddle her butt!"

Boisterous laughter followed. Anna said, "Oh, you girls! What will it be like after a few glasses of wine?"

Chapter 17

ONWARD TO ULITHI

Constantine and Ronnie were successful in getting Eduardo out of the hoosegow. Constantine presented the cash to the jailer for court and signed the promissory note. The court clerk returned Eduardo's passport and he was free to travel. When he was released the following day, he almost ran out of the jail, did a few dance steps like an agile Irishman, and made a dozen promises to Constantine and Ronnie about staying the course on the straight and narrow.

He asked, "My brothers, could we go and get a regular meal at a steak house? For the past four days, I have been eating bland, bland food and tons of rice and fried chicken and fish. I want something green and healthy, something not loaded down with carbohydrates; and I want some hot and tasty spices, maybe some wild boonie peppers."

Constantine smiled and said, "I know just the place. It's the Texas Steak House, with one-pound steaks, and lots of chunky potatoes and onion rings. They have a dozen different types of barbeque and pepper sauces. The salad bar is about forty feet long. You will love it, my little Brother."

Ronnie fired up the rental car and asserted, "No more waiting. I'm famished just hearing about it. This place sounds too good to be true."

The restaurant was spectacular filled with antiques, even an old Indian motorcycle on display, hanging from the ceiling. The food and fresh fruit drinks were delicious and the service sublime. Eduardo glanced secretly at several of the well-endowed waitresses and lithesome patrons. Ronnie noticed, "You're getting healthy. The erotic, black-magic feelings coming back?"

"You caught me. I've forgotten how beautiful women are. They look so soft and feminine. I've been living a life of survival and continually hunting for booze or drugs. No doubt about it – I got all my priorities screwed up. It's good to feel the bodily juices boiling away."

Ronnie said, "And don't forget, they smell good too."

Constantine said, "You clean up and act decent, women will come after you, but don't expect miracles until you get a job and have a proven track record. If you're looking for permanence, the women will want security and long-term commitment. Anything less than that is just a roll-in-the-hay but maybe that's all you want right now. You still have to figure out who you are and where you're trying to go."

Ronnie interjected, "But then, a good woman can help with all that. Helen and I had that for years, but we never spoke out loud. Once we did, we realized marriage was the answer for us."

"Stay focused on sobriety and good things will happen. After our meal, we're going shopping and buy you soaps, shampoos and a toobrush. Your teeth are a strange contrast of yellows."

He closed his mouth and mumbled, "I guess there's no hiding it. I haven't owned a toothbrush in over four years."

Ronnie guffawed and said, "That's going to change right away. You won't be grossing us out with bad breath."

They paid their bill and left a hefty tip, which earned a big smile for Eduardo from the waitress. Ronnie said, "See how it works? Constantine and I are wearing wedding bands. You're not, so you'll be noticed…but the felines won't let you get real close until you brush those teeth. Get some mouthwash too."

Ronnie knew a large department store where they could find hygiene supplies for Eduardo at a good price. Just as they walked inside, a large truck was unloading real Christmas trees, ten-foot blue spruce firs from Oregon, into the garden section. The three men looked at the trees, then each other, and finally Constantine spoke, "Oh yeah, this is going to be good! We're taking a real tree to Yap. It'll be a first."

Eduardo said, "Now Christmas trees are something I know about. I was just reading about them at the shelter. One of the legends about bringing the tree inside goes back to pre-Christian Europe, where the Nordic people believed that fruit trees and evergreens were embodiments of powerful spirits, although there are also other plausible legends. German families in the 16th Century began bringing evergreens into their homes during the holiday season. They were known as *Christbaum* or "Christ trees," and were decorated with fruit, candles and cookies. Of course, when the tree dried, fire from the candles was a real hazard."

"The Christbaum was taken to Great Britain by Queen Victoria's German husband, Prince Albert. The first American trees were brought by German immigrants in the 1829's, but it wasn't until the beginning of the 20th Century that Christmas trees became a popular custom in the United States."

"That's a lot of knowledge for sure," said Constantine.

"Drying out in the rehab was not a complete waste of time… plenty of time for reading."

Halloween and Thanksgiving had passed, but the old stock from the holidays was on sale in the store. Again, Constantine broke the silence, and said, "Muchachos, we will be heroes. We're taking supplies back from the past holidays and for Christmas and New Year's Day, and for my and Andre's birthdays. This is going to be one heck of a big celebration, one that Ulithi will always remember."

Eduardo added, "Papa will love it."

Ronnie said, "And the prodigal son returns. Papa John is going to be one happy man. I'm glad we got some wine for Mother Anna – she does enjoy good wine. That's something she learned on the mainland."

They loaded up two shopping baskets and a twelve-foot tree. Constantine affirmed, "It'll be tough to get all this stuff in the rental car, but wait until they see us at the airport. Going through security is not going to be easy."

Ronnie said, "Yeah, but it's worth it. Let's pack this stuff as tight as we can. Once we get to Ulithi, every kid on the island will want to help unpack."

With help from the store manager, the men managed to get it packed up into various shapes of manageable sizes. The tree would be another matter, relying on the good will of the airport people first, and the agricultural inspectors in Yap. The ticket counter took everything in stride and only charged them a small fee for "over-sized" luggage, that being the Christmas tree. Eduardo's name had been cleared from the commuter on a "detain and arrest" alert, and security was a snap. Through the jet's window, they watched their tree being carefully loaded into cargo. The four-hour plane ride to Yap Proper only had a few bumps but nothing approaching tropical storm or typhoon status.

When they went through the customs and agricultural checks at the Yap International Airport, Constantine merely explained who the tree was for, and that it had been sprayed back on Guam for insidious insects. The two officers were former students of John Sapelalut, and they said that they had heard John had been sick. Constantine explained what was happening with the gathering of the whole family, and how they were going to celebrate six special holidays all at Christmas time.

The Agricultural inspector stated, "Tell your Dad that I wish him well. He was a great teacher – very inspirational. He had to work hard to motivate me but he got me going. I even finished two years of college here on our island."

The Customs man said, "I'm from Asor in the Ulithi Lagoon. Would it be all right if I come over Christmas Day to see your father on Falealop Island? I can crank up my motor boat and pay a visit. I'd like to see him during the holidays."

CHRISTMAS IN THE TROPICS

Constantine answered, "Of course, come over. Should I tell him you're coming?"

"No, no, keep it a secret. I want to surprise him. I'll bring my wife over with our two boys. My wife is a talented cook and she'll prepare something special for the table."

Constantine asked to use the phone. He called down to the harbor and arranged for a launch to take them out to Ulithi the next day. He then called his good friend and canoe builder, Charley Temengue, and made arrangements to visit Charley for the night and talk about a special voyage to Ulithi on Christmas Day. Charley sent a truck to pick them up and bring them out to his home on Maap. The customs man had a friend take their luggage and Christmas tree down to the harbor and load it on the boat for the next day.

Ronnie couldn't help thinking to himself, "Where on the planet can you send off your personal belongings and all the new purchases with a stranger to be loaded on a boat that you haven't seen before or even know the captain of the vessel?" Then he realized he was on Yap, an island of peace and integrity, where the elected politicians and modern legal system is closely monitored by the traditional high chiefs and the cultural mores that have been in place for centuries.

Constantine called Anna and told her the plans for the next day. Papa John was doing fine and had just got up from a long nap. She asked about Eduardo, and let him know also that Belle was really enjoying herself and relaxing. Sweetie was fine also. She asked why he was going to Maap to spend the night. He made up some crazy, fast excuse that he just wanted to see an old friend. He knew that one lie would lead to another. He knew that about his mother.

She asked, "What friend? Who are you going to see?"

He knew if he mentioned Charley, she would know it had something to do with boats and sailing. So he covered it nicely by saying that Ronnie was looking for some unique carvings to take home, and that Maap had some good carvers. That sent her off on another tangent, and she reminded him to look up Johnny and Urbano who were two of her main suppliers for her sales business, both on the internet and to the museums.

Joe Race

Charley greeted them at the village and said he had a special treat lined up for them before the sun set. He and his friend quickly rounded up some gear and took them out in two canoes to go snorkeling and see the manta rays that come in about twilight for feeding on krill. These graceful and peaceful cousins to the shark return day after day to feed and be cleaned of parasites by cleaner wrasses (*Labrus Labridae*) who survive in this symbiotic relationship.

On the short ride out through the crystal-clear water, they saw turtles, moray eels, barracuda, tuna and harmless reef sharks. They slipped over the side of the canoe and swam under the rays and looked up at their silhouettes against the topaz sky. Some of the larger ones had twelve-foot wingspreads, and they noticed that the rays would take turns in swimming into the cleaner stations on the reef. Charley knew some of them by their markings and colors, and names had been given to them (like Spots, Ike, Dude, Lady, etc.) by some of the divers so everyone kind of knew when their favorites were dropping by for a cleaning. The well-known ones had their photos pasted up at most of the dive shops. Several of the larger ones had been featured in *Sports Diver* magazine. Charley wasn't sure this was a good idea and gurgled water through his wind pipe and mask, as he declared, "We're getting too many tourist divers out here now. We might have to limit the numbers and issue permits, just to keep the rays coming back and to protect the coral reefs."

The snorkeling divers noted that there was not one piece of trash bobbing in the waves, including plastic which was ubiquitous, and never dissolving, as in other parts of the ocean.

Even though the moon was bright and the sky clear, the snorkelers swam in before complete darkness fell, pulling the canoes behind them. Charley's wife Marie had dinner prepared. Nothing in the world can compare to fresh-barbequed mahi-mahi, with red hot coconut shells as charcoal, accompanied by fried rice and fresh papaya, while sitting on the beach and watching the final seconds of the falling sun. The ice-cold Japanese Asahi beer complimented the meal beyond belief.

CHRISTMAS IN THE TROPICS

Eduardo good-naturedly bewailed, "I do miss the cold beer. There's just something special about that first cold sip on a hot, humid day."

Constantine firmly said, "Nothing to discuss here, my Little Brother. It's not on your menu…ever!"

Ronnie, being a teetotaler, passed the jug of ice water. "This is mighty good stuff and no calories."

Eduardo responded, "It'll do. Just some old habits to change."

After dinner, Constantine brought up his special plan with Charley and his family.

Charley replied, "Easily done, my Friend. Marie will help with the decorations. No problemo!"

"When does the main canoe get in?"

"Anytime now. Maybe tonight. The master navigator *pwo* is captaining the boat along with Lambert and Alfonso. They're coming all the way from Satawal and I think the extra sailors just came along for the Sapelalut feast. They were his students in elementary school. Besides himself, the captain has to have at least one other crew member just to tack back and forth and to stand the night watch."

Constantine asked, "So you think Matsuo himself is leading the way?"

"Yup, the master navigator himself. He just sailed a canoe all the way from Hawaii to Satawal without a compass or a GPS. The man is becoming world-famous."

"He's the best." Constantine added, "Kammagar, my Amigo. This is going to be great fun for my father."

"Also, like we discussed on the phone, Urbano and Johnny will be over in a few minutes with carvings for Erica, Ronnie and your mother. They carved some sharks, turtles, and dolphins, and even made several outrigger canoe models."

"Good! We gotta haul some handicrafts back to the family to keep the surprise going. I can tell by my mother's voice, she knows something mysterious is going on," said Constantine.

Eduardo reached for the after-dinner tea and concluded, "Nice to be back with the family again. The surprise is going to be so great for Papa."

Ronnie said to Charley, "Please give us some history and details about the Micronesian canoes. They're known everywhere in the sailing community. I'm really curious and I think the canoes and the sailing techniques would make a great story, especially for some of the sailing and historical magazines."

Chapter 18

ANNA REFLECTS

Like any long-term and faithful wife, Anna knew that she would take care and love John until the very end. She wondered what her life would be like without her man and constant companion, and how she would carry on socially and professionally. She was fortunate in that she had her four children, Constantine, Helen, Eduardo and Erica, and their spouses and grandchildren. She had enjoyed raising Andrew and Sweetie, but it appeared that the grandchildren might be going back with their parents full-time. It was so good that Eduardo had regained his life and was coming back to see his Papa.

Anna saw John down at the seashore, sitting in the shade on a long lounge made from local mangrove wood. He was reading a book of his favorite genre, a murder mystery by Robert Parker. She noticed several times that he nodded off, and she thought she should run down and check on him to see if he was okay. But then again, he often nodded off while reading, and if he was gone, there wasn't much she could do for him. He had told her several times that falling asleep along the sea would be nice way to go. He had also told her that he wanted a burial at sea so that he would become part of the cycle of life, be part of the ocean that he loved so much.

She snapped herself out of her gloom and thoughts of death. She remembered that he liked to watch the murder mysteries on television, and that they would guess together who the next victim would be and who was the murderer. Both of them liked to follow the adventures and exploits of the enigmatic Colonel Race and the rotund Belgian detective Hercule Poirot in the Agatha Christie series. She always liked her stories to be tied up at the end with a tidy bow and no questions not answered, like Christie; whereas John preferred an open-ended story with much for the reader to fill in and conclude. John also liked the tough-guy writers like Hemingway, London, and Mickey Spillane. One of her favorite romance writers was Mary Westmacott, which happened to be a pseudonym for Agatha Christie. Both she and John got a great laugh out of this – Anna didn't know about the penname but had noticed some similarities in the writing. A book store manager had told them that Christie and Westmacott were one and the same writer.

While in Guam, Constantine had found two new books for Papa, a "who-dun-it" by Janet Evanovich and a compilation of stories, called "The Best of Mark Twain," both being in the category of Papa's favorite writers. He also told Anna that he had found the latest Toni Morrison book for her, and three complete books in one edition by the Bronte Sisters, Charlotte, Emily and Anne, for Erica. She chuckled to herself when her mainland friends asked what she did to overcome boredom on a remote island, she would hesitate and pretend to be embarrassed by covering her mouth, and almost every time, the female friends would say, "Well, besides that…"

Anna would quickly recover with her friends and say, "We read a lot, so please remember to mail out the books when you've finished. Your used books will get circulated all over the Pacific." As a result, it wasn't unusual to find books in the mail or a swap at the airport, where the owners had written their names inside and listed their home base. Anna had received books from Shanghai, Adelaide, Java, Auckland, Denver, Manila, Bangkok, etc. The first three pages were often covered with names and home addresses. It was also fun to read the quick reviews inside, comments like "really great," "don't waste your time," "use this book to start your next barbeque," "fun, enjoyable reading," "what trash," "the great American novel," and Anna tried not to let the comments influence how she felt about the book. Erica had jokingly told her that anytime a book was marked "smut," "XXX," "garbagio," "should be taken off the shelf," then to bring it to her posthaste.

John and Anna had explored and organized together what would happen when he passed on. They had talked about his burial at sea and put the request and decision in writing so the children wouldn't object. The children would probably expect a regular funeral service with a casket and granite marker. Undoubtedly, that's what the priest would recommend.

They had found all their bank accounts, stocks, insurance policies, retirement plans and policies, deeds, and both had made clearly defined wills, so at the end, there would be no confusion and arguments with the children. Anna stood to control everything until she passed, then Constantine would be the executor for any valuables, land or other parts of the inheritance and it was to be equally divided between the remaining children.

Anna saw that John was awake again, and he was doing his exercises with his arms and legs while sitting in the lounge. His efforts made her feel content. She thought back when he was one of the star baseball players at first base. He was fast and agile, and drove in more homeruns than anyone on his team. He could steal bases like no other. She remembered him being the fastest runner in the 100-meter and 200-meter runs, and how the Palauans and Chamorros would get discouraged when he showed up at a track meet. He would take home most of the gold medals and Yap always scored in the team finals for such a small group of islands.

She also recalled their dating days and what a gentleman he always was. He never wanted to scare her or embarrass her, as he said, "Play the fool with my sweetheart." They both chewed betel nut for awhile, but quit after their teeth started turning dark red, and their breath was bad, and laughingly, she said, "And not good for kissing. If you want a lot of babies, we gotta quit chewing. It's not good for pregnant moms anyway." But she recalled one thing they should have done, being that heart disease ran in his family, was to eat less and take-in only nutritional food, and exercise regularly. They ate a lot of junk and greasy food, bought canned meat and too much barbequed pork, and would often go for weeks without vegetables and fruits, especially when they were on the mainland. They would lay around like "couch potatoes" in between classes for hours and hours watching television or just sleeping.

Anna had discussed all these issues with Constantine, Helen, and Erica, and planned on doing the same with Eduardo. However, Constantine said not to worry about Eduardo because dozens of people had been harping to him about learning to eat right and to exercise and enjoy the sunshine. Thus far, with the exception of Eduardo, none of the children and grandchildren had developed heart disease or diabetes. She had always read nutrition and exercise books and listened carefully to doctors, and her genetics were good, so her health was in the long-living category. Her doctor had told her, discounting an accident or a cancer, that she well live into her nineties. That meant of course, that she would be without John for 25-30 years. It probably wasn't right that a widow should re-marry or go on dates, but she was a vibrant, actually a young sixty years old, woman that enjoyed life.

She saw that John was wide awake and was doing exercises while standing. She thought to herself, what a good time to discuss this issue thing with him. She sincerely felt that being her life companion, that he should have some say in what her future would hold.

She fixed a bowl of fruit and some iced tea, casually strolled down to see John and to start the "widow" discussion.

He saw her coming, and exclaimed, "Here's comes my Sweetie, as beautiful as ever. How come you get prettier and younger?" He paused and gave her a big smile, "And what goodies are on that tray? Something for Papa?"

"Healthy snacks, my Man. You are looking good and doing your exercises. Good for you. Wanna take a walk?"

"In a little while. Let it cool off a bit, besides I've got my eye on those snacks and cold, cold tea."

They ate a little fruit and had their tea. After some small talk about the weather and the flat, quiet sea, Anna decided to go full-bore into what was on her mind. She said, "I love you so much and want you to live forever. But we talked about being real and deciding things before it got confusing or became a problem. The only thing I can't do and you know, if you have a stroke and become disabled, I can't roll you "accidentally into the ocean" and you just end up on the sandy bottom. You already know that, right?"

"Yeah sure, maybe I can persuade Constantine to do it. I don't want to be a continual burden to everyone, including myself. What else? You look real serious."

She stuttered, "Well, I might live for another 20-30 years, and I can't see myself sitting around like a worn-out widow. I would like to get on with life, keep my business and art going. Maybe do some travel."

"Sure, that's great! I don't expect you just to sit down and vegetate, or follow me into the grave. That would be so unfair. I want you to live and be happy! But there's something else, right?"

"Okay, I'll just get out with it. Some of my widow friends stay at home and lead boring lives. They end up dying in a coupla years."

"I don't want that to happen to you."

"Let me finish. This is really hard for me. Some of my other friends, the ones I meet at the senior center, go dancing, play bingo and go out on dates. Some have even remarried."

He laughed and asserted, "So that's what's bothering you, why you look so worried. You have been a wonderful and loyal wife. Why wouldn't I want you to date again? I can't imagine some other old duffer putting his arms around you, but that's life. Loneliness and sitting at home will just destroy your life and make you miserable. You can play with the grandkids for only so long, but then you have to get on with your life."

She looked almost disappointed when she asked, "It would be okay if I dated another man?"

"I wouldn't like it but what's more important is that I want you to feel vital and alive and get on with your life. Turn it around, if you were dying, wouldn't you want me to be happy? You'd probably pick out some good prospects for me and maybe even play matchmaker.

Why is that? Simply because you want me to get on with life and enjoy myself. It wouldn't mean that you loved me any less."

"That's true. It would be a different stage in life. Another plateau. I'd want you to be happy and be with someone."

"Look, it's the same with me. I don't want to sentence you to die, like the outlawed Indian suttee ritual You need to get on with your life, our children, and your interests, and maybe try a few dates. Don't settle for some dirtbag – he has to be the best for my lady!"

She fretted, "I just can't imagine being with another man."

"Relax, you don't have to worry about it for awhile. All the holidays are revving up my whole system. I'm feeling great. I'm ready for a kiss, and our beach walk."

She said, "Thank you. Mahalo for being my husband and such an important part of my life."

"My pleasure, Young Woman."

They kissed, and she pulled him up from the lounge. Off they went, bare feet on sandy beach, like the clock had been turned back to the teenage years.

Chapter 19

VICKY OF TENNESSEE

Vicky Pate's soldier friends weren't surprised by the marriage news but they found it a good reason to celebrate down at the enlisted lounge. They popped a few brewskis, had some very-fattening nachos, and got to tell a lot of romance stories, well some not so romantic. Two of the ladies were married and one, Julie, had received a "Dear Jane" letter the previous week through the email. The husband was at home in Ohio, taking care of their baby, and decided to check out when she told him that she had re-enlisted. It would be an amiable divorce, and the husband promised to care for the baby, and share custody if she ever decided to leave the service. He capped off the letter with a real zinger – he had been lonely for the last several months and had fallen in love with one of their high school classmates, Ella Schmidt.

Julie lamented, "Ella of all people. She was one of those beauty queens, so prissy, and wimpy. Miss Social and about as stuck-up as they come."

Vicky said, "That's what a lot of guys want. They don't want a female jock or a great volleyball player, or in your case, an expert with an M-16 rifle or a gal in training to be a sniper."

Julie concluded, "That's me I guess. I don't wanna be a beauty queen. I just wanna do a great job for the Army."

Rebecca said, "At least you got an email and an explanation. I was living with a guy in Seattle. We had just finished our A.A. Degrees and were deciding what we wanted to do next, like more college or get some jobs. One day when I came home, I noticed most of his stuff was gone. I had been shopping and my arms were full of Christmas food and decorations. My first reaction was a burglar had come in. I was carrying a bottle of wine and I held it like a club to take out the thief. Then I noticed a bright green post-it note on the table. In precise printing, the note said, "Sorry Babe, it's not working out. I'm outa here. Good luck with your life."

"That's cold," Vicky said.

She answered, "Things work out, I suppose. He got busted about a month later for transporting a handgun into Canada by the Canadian customs; then on the way back, the American authorities got him for smuggling a case of Cuban cigars that he planned to sell at the University of Washington. They're not major crimes of course, but it will hurt his chances of being a FBI agent, which was one of his dreams."

The other married lady, Jodi, said, "Sounds like a loser or a guy with real bad luck."

"He's always been that way. 'Bad news' randomness always seems to find him. He's always had the problem of being in the wrong place at the wrong time. But hell, he's gone now. Except one more thing I should tell you, just so you're on the alert for the dogs. For the last two months of our relationship, he was shagging a college history teacher, a woman older than his mother."

Julie smiled, "Now that one makes sense – anything for a good grade."

Rebecca laughed and said, "Well, he did need that class to graduate."

Jodi asked, "And about you, Vicky. How do you feel about the whole thing? Are you happy with the idea of settling down with one man? We've got a whole Army-full of guys to pick from."

"Yeah, I really am. Andre comes from a good family and appears to be honest and sincere. He's been a good soldier and his father is a career First Sergeant and has received dozens of commendations and awards. I've talked to his mother on the phone and she seems very nice."

Julie asked, "How about your family? Are they going to be happy with their precious daughter marrying an island boy and maybe living on a piece of real estate that's a mere speck in a huge ocean?"

"My Mom and Dad are died-in-the wool liberal democrats. They're very open-minded. Dad often professes the theory that drives some of our neighbors into the atmosphere of wackiness when he says the secret to the racial problem is for everyone to mate and intermarry, and then the babies over a few generations would all come out an even shade of grey, kinda like the new president. My folks won't be a problem at all. My Dad will retire in a few years, and they can move to wherever we might be; and then of course, my mom would love to help with the grandbabies. She's a real stay-at-home mom."

Rebecca asked, "Don't you have a brother? How does he feel?"

"Actually Andre and my brother, Joey, have talked a dozen times on the phone. Joey is a career Air Force mechanic and wants to transfer to Guam for the fishing and diving. Andre promises to show him the best dive spots in Micronesia. So if we end up on Guam or Saipan for college, then Joey would be there."

Rebecca continued, "Sounds like you've thought it through. So how are you going to convince the sergeant that you're not going to re-enlist? He's going to throw a $25K bonus at you and probably a promotion in rank."

"Won't be a problem. I'll be thinking of my sweet macho-man and our life together. Hot doggie!"

Jodi smiled, "Good for you, but just watch out for those 'adios' emails and post-it notes."

Julie added, "And keep him away from the high school beauty queens."

"Messages received. Thank you, Ladies. Now, let's have another Corona!"

They raised and clinked their glasses. Jodi said, "To men, the bastards! May we keep going after them."

Rebecca added, "A necessary evil! You girls just don't interest me that way."

Vicky spoke to André two days later and confirmed that they were both on track for not re-enlisting. She then worked up her nerve and explained to the First Sergeant that she was planning on leaving the service and getting married. He lackadaisically went through the motions about getting her to stay on and explained the bonus, probably a promotion and a new job assignment (which could easily be Iraq or Afghanistan). The sergeant knew that most of the re-enlistment sessions would be unsuccessful – only about twenty per cent of the soldiers were re-enlisting, mainly because of the futility and politics of the war, and they home. She declined his offer and then passionately told him about her upcoming wedding and their college plans. He understood, saying he missed his wife and family terribly.

"Where's this Yap anyway. I've never heard of it, probably we haven't had a war there yet."

"Actually Ulithi, where my fiancée is from, was a major military staging area for the northern advances on Japan in World War II. Also just a few hundred miles way is Peleliu in Palau. This was one of the islands that General Macarthur decided to conquer while advancing and returning to Manila. It was a nasty battle on both sides."

The First Sergeant asked, "When was your last leave?"

"Over a year ago. We've been pretty busy in the Comm. Center."

"Listen, I've got three new corporals coming in next week. There are other operators that can train them."

"What are you saying?"

"I've been bit by the "Goodwill Bug" and think maybe you should take a month's leave at Christmas time. You've been working hard and maybe you need to see that man of yours, and especially your new island home. I just can't imagine a city girl like you living in a grass hut with a sandy floor and constantly under attack by gnats and mosquitoes...and pigs and chickens running in and out of the front door."

"I love the photos, and the way he describes everything."

"Hey, some people like living in Downtown LA or Detroit. You better go take a look at it before you sign the papers."

CHRISTMAS IN THE TROPICS

"When can I leave?"

"In a coupla days. But tell the other soldiers that the leave came through from headquarters. I don't want them to think the old Sarge has gone soft."

"Thank you, Sarge. I'm just betting you have a daughter about my age."

"Two of them. They made me a Grandpa. I miss the whole mob! Now, get out of here and start packing."

"I'm going to surprise everybody on my leave. I'm just going to pop in to see my folks in Tennessee, spend a few days catching up on the home news, and then off to Guam and Yap. Then I'll just casually call Andre from the airport and ask for a boat ride to his island. He's going to be so surprised and excited."

"Get moving lickety-split! You've got a soldier boy waiting to see your pretty face, and this time without sweat and camouflage paste. Ditch the Army-issue cotton underwear, and wear some girly perfume so you don't smell like gun-cleaning fluid and diesel fuel."

"Copy that, Sarge! Yep, I'm off to Paradise."

Chapter 20

DOC AND FAMILY

As promised, Doctor Hilario Carter opened up a family discussion about a trip to Yap for the Christmas holidays with his wife, Barbara, and their two teenage daughters Hillary and Sarah. There was no hesitation about going the islands from the oldest daughter Hillary, but Barbara and Sarah were reluctant to leave all their friends and family at such a special time of year. Barbara said, "Christmas means family and loved ones, and evergreen trees and snow. It means icicles hanging from the eaves and it makes us want to run inside and sit in front of big fireplace with a roaring fire and drink hot apple cider with cinnamon."

Doc surmised, "Yeah, but we're always talking about doing different things and having an adventure. What could be better? We have a great contact with my Yapese patient and his family. They are delightful people. We can still see our friends and family before and after the holidays, and that would extend the holidays, which you girls should appreciate. If you like, we could be home for New Year's Eve."

Hillary exclaimed, "I'm already in. You don't have to convince me. I want the adventure and meeting new people, especially native people living way out in the Pacific. They must be so interesting, living in that environment."

CHRISTMAS IN THE TROPICS

"My patient John Sapelalut left me a disc with about one hundred pictures of Yap, including the outer islands. Let's take a look on the computer screen – maybe I can convince you other two ladies that we should go. I've looked at them twice and see something different each time."

After twenty minutes and several dozen "oohs" and "ahhs," Sarah asked, "You say we can get certified for diving out there and the water's about eighty degrees? I could go spear fishing?" She was starting to switch sides. The 50-50 count was starting to change but Barbara still needed some convincing.

Barbara concluded at the end of the slide show, "Let me think about it overnight. I know my parents are going to Europe for their special trip, and your folks have talked about taking a holiday cruise to Mexico. So maybe, we can all get together for a big New Year's party. I know I'm outvoted three to one, but hey, I'm the mom. My votes are worth at least three points, so that makes us even again."

Hillary sighed, and the daughters wandered off to bed. Doc asked, "Barbie-Doll, wanna watch the slides again?"

"Okay, one more time."

"Now, while you're watching, think of the peace and tranquility of lying on a sandy beach, and the warm, tropical breezes. Visualize the full moon reflecting over the silver sea, leaving a shiny trail right to your blanket, and if you listen real hard, you can hear the palm fronds sending soft electric signals to massage your naked skin."

"You are some kind of talented poet. You make it so tempting… and sensuous."

"That's because is it is sensuous and hypnotizing. Remember our trip to Belize and how you hated to leave? It got so quiet at nighttime on the beach, that every time there was a loll in the waves, you said that you could actually hear your heartbeat. In your own poetic feeling, you whispered, "I am one with earth, a sweet surcease from ordinary to a special spiritual place."

"That was poetic wasn't it?"

"Sure, and don't you want to experience it again? You remember how sexy you felt?"

"Oh yeah! You convinced me. I'll go on the trip, but don't tell the girls yet. While they're convincing me to go, they'll be working out their own decisions, like leaving their best friends for two weeks. That's a big decision for a teenage girl." She smiled and hugged Doc, and uttered, "Yap, wherever you are, here we come!"

The daughters needed no convincing next morning.

The preparations for Yap went smoothly. Doc had already arranged for other physicians to cover his rounds and do the follow-up with his patients. The travel agency went to work on the tickets, and of course, the first reaction was, "Where is Yap?" Doc knew which airlines went to the remote islands, and he referred the agency clerk to Continental Airlines. Again, another exclamation, "Wow, Continental knew about Yap and Guam. Out in the islands they call their flights Continental Micronesia."

Barbara and their daughters started packing like they were going on a four-week voyage through coldest Siberia. Doc decided to parrot what John had to say about clothes, "Bring some shorts and tops, a few pair of flip-flops and sandals, and some sunscreen, plus your normal toiletry kit. You won't need much, and we can supply all the dive and snorkeling equipment. Tell your daughters we have spear guns and regular six- foot spears to use on the reef."

Doc spoke to John on the phone several times. He cleared up one thing right away that his female family members were worried about. They had read on the internet that the local women go topless and besides the modesty issues, they were concerned about bug bites and sunburn. Doc wasn't sure that he would be comfortable in a thu with his white backside hanging out. John assured them they could dress the way they normally do at home but the ladies had to wear long skirts or lava-lavas to cover their thighs, which were considered extremely sensual to the local males.

John added, "Other than that, bring a huge appetite. The fishing has been really good. My cousins caught three large barracudas yesterday."

"How about sleeping arrangements?"

"We have a thatched hut fixed for you. My relatives constructed it where there's a nice breeze and not many bugs. You'll have a fantastic view of the sunrise. Also I have a dog that can watch over you in case anyone comes walking around at night, and he'll also watch your belongings while you're away."

"It there a thief or night prowler problem? If so, the girls won't like that."

"Nope, nothing like that. Just a precaution. Nothing to worry about."

John asked Doc to bring all their old DVD movies that they had viewed several times for circulation on Ulithi, and also any extra books that they might have. The boys were into action movies, and of course, the local girls liked cartoons and love stories. The daughters had already packed some their clothes that they had out-grown and also their old toys and dolls for the younger island children.

Doc took an order from Anna for the medicines that were running short for John's condition. He said that he and his family would be heading out in a few days, with a two-day stopover in Hawaii, one of their favorite places, and then two-days in Guam, and then on to Yap. John said that someone would be at the airport to pick them up, and get them to the launch that would bring them to Ulithi.

Doc hugged Barbara and their daughters and said, "Ladies, we are island-bound. We are heading for the tropical islands, the land of wonder, serenity and mango trees. We won't be counting time in seconds, minutes or hours, just living from sunrise to sunset, like a human was meant to do. No watches and no hassles."

Barbara chuckled and said, "Oh Great Surgeon, will we also experience more poetry?"

"Oh yes. We will experience rainbow hues and the ocean's blues, and enjoy those velvet nights and crazy delights, and explore the dark jungle lands and journey to the sun-bleached strands." He paused and guffawed, "And ladies, that is only the beginning of this poet's extensive creativity...and his silliness. We will have fun!"

Hillary smiled, "Sure sounds like it. He's a poet and we don't know it!"

"Hey, give your poor old Dad a break...!"

Chapter 21

THE FLYING PROA

The sailing craft of Micronesia have long attracted the attention of sailors all over the world. Sitting around a beach fire in front of his own canoe, Charley gave Constantine, Ronnie and Eduardo a quick lesson about the evolution of the island type of outrigger sailing canoe that is of an efficient design radically different than western craft. Many of the canoes throughout the Pacific Region bare a family resemblance and differences are mainly attributable to local factors. The canoe has been instrumental in the various islands communicating and trading, and of course, for enabling the islands to enjoy subsistence fishing.

The most efficient of the sailing canoes is the "flying proa" of the Caroline Islands, including Yap. In early days the canoes impressed voyagers such as Magellan, because of their speed and agility, and because they can change stern and bow at will, and resemble fun-loving dolphins skipping over the waves. Changing front to back, or reverse is the unique way in which the canoe is sailed. The Yapese proa is called a *popo* which is built-up from a dugout keel to which are attached carefully fitted strakes. The hull-forming strakes are secured with sennit twine and the seams are caulked with sennit fibers and tree gum. Outrigger booms attach to the topmost strakes on each side of the hull and extend eight to ten feet to from the weather side. The outrigger float is solid wood and is shaped for little water resistance. The weight of the outrigger is as important as it it's buoyancy; when moving fast under sail, the float often is raised clear of the water, and this weight counters the canoe's heeling tendency. *Popos* usually have about a 9.4meter heel length and the length of the booms to the axis of the float, about 3.5 meters. The length of the float is about four meters.

Ronnie asserted, "Charley, you're losing me already. It's more complicated than I thought."

Eduardo said, "I always thought it was so simple."

Charley stated, "That's what makes a big deal, sailing across the Pacific without instruments, and just a dug-out tree between you and elements. You have to be thinking all the time."

He continued by accounting that the sail is the shape of an isosceles triangle with the two longer edges laced to two long poles. The mast is shorter than these spars, and pivots fore and aft from the middle of the hull. Inside there is a platform used for cargo and passengers. There is often a low hut of woven palm frond on top for protection from the weather. If there are more passengers than one hut can accommodate, then another can be built on the float booms, between the hull and the float. There are variations in design and markings and a seasoned sailor can determine a canoe's place of origin by its appearance and construction techniques The huts might be different, boom size and application, frames fitting into the hull, and design of the floats.

Charley said, "There is a writer named Hornell that said there is no finer design of a canoe than that of the Micronesians, primarily for three reasons:

1. *The flattened lee side of the hull acting as a leeboard to reduce drift to leeward and compensating to some extent for the pull to the weather side of the outrigger float;*
2. *The use of a lee platform on the cantilever system, enabling a greater quantity of cargo to be carried;*
3. *The midships pivoting of the mast, where the canoe was able to sail either end forward and so to keep the outrigger on the weather side, whichever course she was on."*

Charley continued by stating that when sailing, the wind is always kept on the outrigger side. If the wind came over the flat side, the canoe would be taken aback and as the mast is not supported from that flat side, it could be dismasted. A steersman works a large steering paddle from the extreme stern of the hull. Another crew member controls the sheet. To tack an outrigger it takes at least two persons. Micronesian canoes sail easiest across the wind or somewhat downwind. A wind change could easily result in a gust from the wrong side that would capsize the canoe, and because upwind sailing will subject the craft to greater stress. There is a long list of taboos and rituals associated with canoe building and sailing, which sometimes causes problems for the sailors. For example, the captain of a sailing canoe would not ever think of going to sea without a sacred bracelet made of certain types of coral, which symbolizes "toughness" in the face of adversity. Other beliefs seem outdated in that only "vegetable matter" be used to secure certain parts of the boat, when metal screws and nuts and bolts might be more efficient and would last longer.

Constantine asked, "You really tout the Flying Proa as being efficient and still kinda modern. What are some of the advantages and disadvantages?"

"We've already talked about a lot of advantages. The asymmetrical hull resist leeward drift without the depth or drag of a keel and it is aerodynamical design allows it to shoot over the water like the flow of an aircraft wing. The weight of the outrigger float performs the same function as a lead keel but the ability of its weight to counter wind pressure is immediate because it is attached at 90 degrees to the mast. It's designed to go fast and be light on the water."

Ronnie asked, "Disadvantages?"

Charley continued, "There is a lot of manhandling of the sail from one end to the other, and the boat can't be sailed single-handed. The sail being attached so fat forward causes the lee helm tending to turn the canoe downwind when trying to tack. When running before the wind, the sail thrust is all outboard of the flat side and the float is in the water dragging on the other side. This necessitates the use of a large steering paddle to keep it on course, which constitutes a drag."

CHRISTMAS IN THE TROPICS

Constantine asked, "What would be the best way to go then?"

"An ideal design should provide a canoe that can be worked single-handed, including moving the rig from one end to the other. Either the sail plan to the center of lateral resistance should be continuously adjusted for steady tacking upwind, and to lessen the need for a heavy rudder or paddle when sailing off the wind. There should be a way to spill the excess wind."

Ronnie chuckled, "It's always a good design when you don't have to buy smelly, expensive gasoline."

Eduardo laughed and said, "Sailing these flying proa is probably more than I can ever learn or understand. Did you make the 'master navigator' class? Your cousins tell you sail all over the lagoon and into the open sea."

"Yeah, there's a lot to learn. I sure wouldn't to try a run to Saipan or Tahiti. I'm not even close to attaining any rank in the Hawaiian based Polynesian Voyaging Society. The other association is called the Weiyeng School of Navigation which began on Pollap Island. First you become a *paliuw* Master Navigator and the ultimate level is *pwo*. The last induction ceremony was held right on Satawal Island of Yap State. Our friend Matsuo, who will be sailing with us, has been inducted as *pwo* status.

Chapter 22

━━━━━

BACK HOME – EDUARDO

Constantine, Ronnie and Eduardo finished their arrangements with Charley at Maap Village, and were homeward bound to beautiful, remote Ulithi. Charley gave them a fresh fifty-pound yellow fin tuna as a special present to John, and to remind him to come to Colonia once in awhile so they could go snag some big ones in the open ocean.

The lads went to the launch as planned, and the Captain was there and had the boat checked up and full of fuel. He also had some fishing lines tied on the back of the launch for some trolling if they happened to see a large flock of birds. If the birds were circling, that meant the smaller fish were being driven to the surface by larger predators underneath. It always reminded Constantine that sometimes life doesn't give you many choices, like the smaller fish taking a chance on being eaten below or coming to the surface and then being attacked by the birds. Of course, he chuckled to himself, the little ones might get a break as they were trolling under the birds and the larger predator fish went for their lures.

About an hour out of the harbor, good fortune came their way and after making four passes under the circling birds, they had about two hundred pounds of albacore and mahi-mahi to feed their extended family for a week. Eduardo worked right alongside his brothers catching the fish, and then cleaning and packaging. Constantine noticed that he was taking on normal skin color – he was going from pasty light brown to his normal chestnut hue. The lads called it a day, pulled in their fishing gear, and headed straight for Ulithi.

Constantine cut up some fresh fish and made *finadene* (soy, peppers, vinegar), and they snacked on fresh sashimi and ate from a basket of mangos and pineapple that the Captain had brought aboard. Just another typical meal on the open seas in the blue, blue Pacific.

There was a large welcoming group waiting for them on reaching John's beach. Eduardo and John had direct eye contact and were waving at each other. Anna was close to tears, seeing that her youngest son made it back home safely. Once anchored, Eduardo jumped off into the shallow surf and went directly to his father. They hugged, and then he turned to his mother, and they hugged. He was welcomed back into the family. Then there was a quick commotion of everybody chattering and hugging at the same time, Helen with Ronnie and Constantine with Belle. It was joyous.

Eduardo said to his father and mother, "I'm so sorry for what I did to you both, and how I shamed the family. Please forgive me. I'm recovering now, thanks to all my family members."

Eduardo's son Andrew was peeking out from the bushes. He was holding back to see what his father was really like. Anna said, "Not to worry – it'll work out. He'll come out when he's ready."

John said, "You're forgiven. Let's walk up to the house. I'm a little weary right now. It's so good to see you at home and that you're back on the right track. It's going to a special, memorable Christmas."

Eduardo winked at Helen, "Any good-looking girls left on the island?"

"You must be getting better, thinking about the ladies again. I thought you had given up romance for drugs."

"Oh, I was real dopey once, but no more. Answer my question, please."

"I know a coupla prospects. You have to realize at our ages, most of the ladies have children, so it would be a package deal. No way a good mother will abandon her children."

"No problem there. I wouldn't have much faith in a gal if she was willing to dump her children for an ex-doper."

"I'll ask around and see if someone would like to drop over later. Do you remember Florencia from school? Her husband ran off with a young girl abut four years ago and left her with three kids. She still looks good, very slender and svelte, and supports herself by making handicrafts for our mother."

"Yeah, I remember her. She was a real beaut."

"Do you think she'd come over to see me?"

"I think so. She's asked about you several times. If she doesn't come over, go over and see her. She doesn't have a boyfriend, so you don't have to worry about getting clunked on the head by a mangrove club."

He smiled, "I hope she comes over tonight."

"Me, too. You'd make a good-looking couple."

"This is more exciting than drugs. It makes me feel alive again."

Helen added, "And it's only beginning, Lover Boy."

Eduardo's welcome home party was a small affair, everyone waiting on the island to see if he had really turned his life around. Most of the village remembered him being drunk and acting stupid all over the village, and being disrespectful to the elders. They were also playing the wait-and-see game to see if he would re-start his marijuana packaging and sales business to visiting yachties or move his stock of drugs over to Yap Proper for his sales. Most of the tourists never got to Ulithi, so anything that a person wanted to sell to tourists it had to be distributed in or near Colonia, both legal and illegal wares.

John and Anna loved their son unconditionally, but in the past he had proven a headache for them and a definite embarrassment for Yap. But they were willing to give him every chance to clean up his act and become a good citizen. Thus far, he had been a gentleman, and helped the family wherever he could. Constantine reassured them that he would be fine, that when he hit bottom the brain cells lit up bright and clear about his future.

During the dinner on Helen's invitation, Florencia and her three delightful children, ages four, six, and eight, arrived for dinner. All

CHRISTMAS IN THE TROPICS

the little ones had their own picnic table so Eduardo and Florencia had a chance to talk with the adults and to get to know each other. His first reaction to himself was simply, "Why would such a gorgeous woman even notice me, let alone sit down and talk to me?"

But she did sit and chat with him and enthusiastically. Once she found that he was safe to talk to and a nice person, she opened up and reminisced about their high school days. She remembered that he had been pleasant to her even when he was drinking or smoking too much. She had been one grade behind him and had a secret crush on him all through school. They sat on a blanket under a spreading island pandamus tree bearing huge fruit.

When he became a doper, she knew there wasn't a future for her and she had married a hard-working farmer who for the first years of their marriage had been loving and a good provider. But as time went by, he grew discontented with farming and when he tried college, he found that it was too much of a challenge. He was restless and when a young neighbor girl started flirting with him and wanted to go to the mainland, he was off like a rocket, leaving a hurt, confused wife and three hungry children in his wake.

Basically the husband was out of the picture, and Florencia had only one short-term affair with an educator. But that had run its course in a few months. She knew that her children's presence was the reason he had left – he just wasn't ready to make a commitment to four people. He had been an only child and had never had children of his own and just wasn't up to the demands and the responsibilities. The noise and commotion bothered him. He didn't just disappear like the husband. They talked long and hard, and finally they decided to part as friends. He took a job in Chuuk and she hadn't seen him since the break-up. There had been no follow-up emails or phone calls.

Eduardo said that he had noticed her in their school years but she seemed way out of his league for dating. She was smart and popular. He explained his love life with a real person was zero, jokingly saying he had been in love with Mary Jane (marijuana), had a fling with Snow Girl (cocaine), ran away with Speedy Sally (amphetamines) and spent too time with Hazy Lady (opiates)...and reminded her that he took a long vacation with Boozy Lucy (wine, whisky and tequila). He said that he couldn't ever recall having a real date with any girl or woman. He asked that she excuse him, scold him, or train him, if he was awkward, boorish or irritating, because he had never been properly "house-broke" by his mother or auntie, or a real girlfriend. He hadn't developed social skills during his doper years.

She said, "You're doing just fine. Just relax and be yourself. I like who you are. If you act like someone that you're not, it'll show through real fast. No body likes phonies."

He chuckled and exclaimed, "What you see is what you get."

"I like what I see."

"You know about my son Andrew, right? My mother raised him when his birth mother ran off to Guam. And I sure wasn't any help."

"Of course I know about Andrew. He plays with my children all the time, especially the eight-year-old."

"I'm going to make him and my parents proud, go to college, and get a job. I wanna make this Christmas so special for everyone in the family. This holiday season is extra meaningful. My rehabilitation is what Christmas means to me."

"Sounds exciting and fulfilling. I hope you don't get lonely."

"If I can you see you every once in awhile, I'll be fine."

"How about we partner up if you stay on the straight and narrow?"

"You'd be willing to help me…pay attention to me?"

"Sure thing."

"But I'm an old broken-down drunk."

"No more. You told me yourself."

Chapter 23

CHRISTMAS EVE PLANNING

Anna planned the Christmas Eve dinner early so that John would be wide awake and ready to celebrate with everyone. The mainland Christmas tree was a big hit. And once again, the ladies had prepared a scrumptious meal. The padre blessed the food and reminded everyone about the real meaning of Christmas, and about the upcoming Christmas service in the morning at beachside. The children sang several traditional Yapese and American songs, and the seniors did a slow leisurely rhythmatic dance with Anna calling out the movements. The gifts wouldn't be opened until the following morning, after Santa had made his deliveries from his canoe.

The family member had contributed to a huge stack of fireworks, including rockets and giant, colorful fireworks bursting in the air. The islands were green and moist and there wasn't a danger of fire. Most of the rockets were shot out over the lagoon. The adult members of the family did the lighting and the children got to sit back and enjoy the noise and flaming colors, and play with their sparklers. After the fireworks display, the teenagers built a massive bonfire and people sat around on the sand and talked about previous holidays seasons, where they had been and what they were doing and with whom. John loved hearing the old campfire songs that had been passed down through the generations.

John soon grew weary and asked Anna to take him to bed. He laughed and giggled all the way through his sponge bath. She fixed his medication and made him comfortable.

He said, "If this is what Heaven is like, I'm ready to go."

"Not yet, Lover Boy. You still have a lot of living to do." They kissed and she laid her head across his abdomen until he was fast asleep. She heard a knock on the door.

Erica asked, "Are you awake? May I come in?"

Anna whispered back, "Sure, come in."

"If Papa is asleep, can you come out. The family wants to talk to you."

"I'm on the way. Papa is fine. His breathing is steady, and he's zonked after all the festivities."

When she reached the outside kitchen area, she found the whole family sitting on and around the picnic tables. Everyone appeared to be on pins and needles with excitement. They were all laughing and the children jumping for joy.

She asked, "Okay, what is it. What's going on?"

Several of the family members told Constantine to explain. He said, "Mother, we have a magnificent surprise for Papa. We're all going to rendezvous just inside the reef on canoes and boats."

"What are you talking about. Who's 'we? Who else knows about this?"

"All the family and loads of Papa's friends. Look around the lagoon at the other islands. Do you see any lights going out? You know why? Everyone is getting organized and ready to meet about three kilometers from here."

"Then what?"

"We'll sail in together, waving banners and singing Christmas carols. He'll love it. You can sail out with us, and then back in. We have some of the well-known Yapese sailors and major canoes leading the way."

Anna looked worried, "I can't leave your father. He might need me in the night, or first thing in the morning."

CHRISTMAS IN THE TROPICS

"Not to worry. Helen and Erica are going to stay on island, and Doc will be here back in his grass shack. His family is going with us on the boats. We've got it covered."

"Okay then.   Let me get some things together. How about the children; they'll need blankets and they'll fall asleep on the boats because it's so late. And don't forget their life preservers."

Helen said, "All done. All take care of."

Andre received a telephone call. His first response was, "Who would be calling way out here? Hope it's not from Iraq and our leave has been cut short."

The caller said, "Andre, this is Charley, your dad's friend in Maap. Got someone here that wants to talk to you. She's jumping up and down."

A voice came on. It was Vicky, all the way from Germany; but Andre was momentarily confused. He thought he heard from Charley that Vicky was there. But it was Vicky and her beautiful, sweet voice.

She said, "Hi, Darling. It's me. Merry Christmas!"

Andre covered the mouthpiece on the phone and yelled out to everyone, "Hey, Family. You won't believe this but my fiancée is here in Yap State." The family applauded, and then in unison, wished her "Happy Holidays."

He spoke again on the phone. "The family excited about meeting you. So how are we going to get you here for Christmas Day? Got a plan yet?"

"Charley told me that he just load me on with Mau in one of the two canoes and we'd sail out tonight. They tell me the weather is cooperating."

"Good, get here soon. There's supposed to be a large tropical storm brewing out east of us, but it'll take a day to get here, so you folks will be fine. If I know those sailors, they don't have sophisticated weather and electronic gear with them."

She laughed, "I asked about that and they pooh-poohed my question and asserted, 'why waste money when you can look at the stars and the moon.' I don't think they watch the Weather Channel so I'm throwing caution to the fates, and depending on the sailors totally. Charley tells me it will be fine."

Andre laughed and asked, "Have you got used to the *thus* yet, and are you ready to go topless?"

Vicky answered, "Topless doesn't bother me. I'm still a young lass. But I've never seen so many butts in my life. I never knew there so many shapes."

He chuckled and said, "See you soon my Darling. Everyone is waiting to meet you, especially my mother. But my father gave you the super OK, so Mom will be a cinch. Now, can you put Charley back on the line?"

Andre went over the plans again with Charley. He said everything was set, that Mau was getting ready to cast off. He added, "I'm coming along in my canoe. I've never had the nerve to go onto the open ocean before, but I figured with Mau along, I'd be fine. He's also putting Alphonso, one of the experienced guys, on board with me in case we get separated. But I'm doing a little cheating. I'm taking along my ship-to-shore emergency radio, just in case I really get separated and can't find Mau, or vice-versa. I can get in contact with the police and emergency services, and then get patched through to the coast Guard."

"Good then. We've got the plan going. Grandpa is going to be really surprised. We're about to leave here and then get together with the neighbors near the west end of the lagoon."

Constantine listened to the end of the phone call, and gathered up the family members and said to jump in the canoes and the motor launch.

Sweetie came over to Constantine and Belle and asked, "Would be okay with you if I stayed here with Aunties Erica and Helen, just in case Grandpa needs something. Besides I want to see his face and take his photo in the morning with my digital camera, when all the boats start turning up."

Constantine looked at Belle and she nodded her approval.

"Mommy says it okay. I'm glad you love your grandparents. They've done a good job raising you."

CHRISTMAS IN THE TROPICS

She chuckled, "Yes Daddy, I'm just a little angel." She curtsied.

Constantine smiled and waved goodbye.

As the boats shoved off from the shore, Sweetie yelled out, "Merry Christmas. See you soon."

Helen and Erica swung their lanterns back and forth. Doc sat on a bench, shooting the beam of his flashlight into the sky. He was kinda slouched over.

Helen asked, "Why so sad-looking, Doc?"

"I guess I'm thinking about your father, how he will miss her family and you will miss him every day. My family is only going a few kilometers in the lagoon and I already miss them."

Erica answered, "It's tough for all of us. We'll miss him. He's been the one, reliable rock in my life, my safe place. He was always strong and reliable, and a man of honor and integrity. Crime could be rising and the stock market crashing, but we could always go home and find comfort. And I enjoyed watching the continuous love affair between Mother and Papa."

Helen said, "I believe in immortality. He will always be with us, maybe not in body but in spirit and every decision we make and do. He raised us with a strong personal code – kinda like the Ten Commandants and the Golden Rule, and the teachings of Buddha, about honesty and kindness."

Doc said, "He will leave a wonderful legacy."

Erica got them back on track, "Hey, Papa is not dead. He's with us for Christmas. It's a very special time for all of us!"

Doc added, "You're so right!"

Helen said, "Amen to that."

A soft little voice said, "You shouldn't all worry. Grandpa is going to Heaven. I know he will," said Sweetie, who hadn't missed a word of the conversation.

Chapter 24

―――――

THE CHRISTMAS FLOTILLA

The rendezvous went according to schedule and location. The fishermen in the lagoon were not necessarily master navigators or sailors but they knew their lagoon and how to coordinate meeting spots. They would often get together in the middle and exchange news about the other islands, drink a glass of *tuba* (fermented coconut) and swap some fish. Some fishermen were unlucky and came up empty but they all had children who had married into other clans, including the Sapelaluts, so there was always some type of familial obligation. The ones with the empty boats would often drop by later in the week with a load of pineapples, bananas, papayas, betel nut, or mangos. Events and exchanges always seemed to work out and everyone had food on the table.

The sea was quiet, and the boaters were able to tie up close with each other, and the occupants could walk from boat to boat without using a dinghy, or getting wet and swimming to the other boats. Charley had made the voyage without a complication and there was grand reunion between Vicky and Andre. He introduced her to his mother, who hugged her and said, "Please call me Mother." Belle winked at André, and whispered, "She's a beauty, you lucky man."

Andre stood on one of the huts on Matsuo's canoe and said, in a loud voice, "My family and friends, this is my Vicky, soon to be my wife. We're both soldiers right now, but after a few months, we will be plain old civilians and looking for a chance to go to college. We may hang out in the islands for a few months just to decompress and get used to sleeping past six o'clock in the morning. So when you see her walking around or boating around the lagoon, she's not an outside teacher, at least not yet, or a Peace Corps rep, she's my wife and a member of the Sapelalut family. Please treat her with love and care."

Constantine led the family and friends in a "hip-hip-hooray" and Vicky was traditionally welcomed into the family. She would never again worry about finding a meal or a place to sleep, or need protection from "bad guys" when she was in the islands. She was protected and loved. She had joined the families of the Ulithi lagoon.

Matsuo calculated the distance to the Sapelalut beach, and said that it would be a thirty-minute ride and they would reach shore just as the sun was peeking up from the east. He would lead the flotilla with the family members in the stern. Charley's wife had decorated the two large canoes with glowing lights and banners. Anna organized the songs to be sung and said to follow her directions. She had decorated a long bamboo baton to look like a bright red and white candy cane.

There were at least another thirty boats and canoes of all sizes and designs that would follow Charley and Matsuo's canoes. There was plenty of wind, the right pressure to move the canoes at a steady pace. Just before sunrise, the flotilla began to move towards the beach. They could lights see coming on at the Sapelalut house and outbuildings.

In the main house, John awoke and reached for Anna to give her a good-morning kiss. She was gone. He just figured she got up a little early to make coffee and get the breakfast going for the whole family. She always made a special Christmas breakfast, which usually included pancakes and cinnamon rolls and large plate of crispy bacon. He knew they weren't on his diet, but knowing Anna, she probably fixed them for him and would allow a little leeway on such a special day.

The sun was rising through the white fluffy clouds on the horizon. The birds were cheerfully chirping and the palms were swaying with a warm, gentle breeze. It was a typical morning on Ulithi. John recalled the noise and craziness of the morning commute in Honolulu, and appreciated his beach even more.

When he walked out onto the beach, he saw children running everywhere looking for gifts left by Santa when he had landed his canoe in the night. He saw Helen and Erica smiling, and they gestured over to some of the smaller coconut trees. Sweetie was busily digging away in the fronds and finally found two brightly-wrapped gifts with her name on top. He didn't see Andrew. He thought it unusual, as Andrew was typically the first one up on Christmas Day.

Doc was in the outside kitchen building a large pot of coffee. John didn't see Anna or see any baking or cooking in the kitchen. He walked over to Erica and asked, "Okay, Baby Girl. What's going on? Where's Mother?" Helen walked away sniggering, knowing that she had evaded her Papa's direct questioning.

Erica stuttered, "Nothing going on, Papa. Mother just took an early walk on the beach."

Within a few minutes, the children started screaming about boats on the west side of the lagoon. One of the neighbor boys excitedly said, "There's gotta be a hundred boats coming. Maybe Santa's coming back."

In amazement, Papa asserted, "He's right. I've never seen that many boats at one time. Most of them are under sail, that's why we didn't hear them before. That's a lot of boats. Wonder what they're doing way out there?"

Helen came out with Papa's binoculars and said, "Take a look. See anybody you know?"

"I can't believe it. It's Mother right in front, and there's Constantine and Belle, and now I see Eduardo and our neighbor Florencia and her kiddies. I see Ronnie and there's Andre, and he's got his arm around some foreign girl."

Erica said, "She won't be a foreign girl much longer. I think that's Andre's fiancée. They going to get married as soon as they're out of the Army."

CHRISTMAS IN THE TROPICS

Papa said, "Now I see Andrew. He's jumping around like a monkey and he's smiling big-time. I think the morning sun is reflecting of his white teeth."

Helen had rounded up some white plastic chairs and took them down to the waterline. Erica took Papa by the arm and guided him to the chairs. She said, "Let's take it easy and wait for the boats, and see what they're doing. Maybe they had a big fishing derby."

Papa chuckled and said, "If that's the case, they must have cleaned out the lagoon with all those boats."

Helen asked, "See anyone else you know? Maybe like who the overall captain seems to be?"

He adjusted his binoculars and exclaimed, "I see Matsuo, the master navigator of all the islands. I knew him from Satawal. Now, I see Mother starting to gather the children and put them out front."

When the boats were fifty yards off shore, Papa heard one of his favorite Christmas songs, "Santa Claus is Coming to Town," then as the boats neared shore, everyone on all the boats started singing "Oh Come all Ye Faithful." Papa stood and applauded when the hymn finished.

Constantine stood in front of the Matsuo's canoe, and said, "Papa, this for you. You wanted the family together for Christmas and here we are, plus all your friends and neighbors. We wish you a Merry Christmas." Everyone then sang "We Wish You a Merry Christmas," the music surrounding the jungle. Everyone on shore joined in, including Papa who fumbled through the words, like he hadn't sung since being a child.

The children took the ending of his song as a cue, and they soon were jumping over the sides of the boats and wading and swimming to shore. Then, with Constantine leading off, the adults jumped into the 85-degree water and the entire group, shaking off the water like a pack of gleeful dogs, surrounded John on the beach. There were a lot of hugs and kisses, but the most memorable was when John kissed Anna and said, "Thank you, my Darling Girl. I love you for all of this, and love you more every day. Thank you, thank you!"

John then addressed the crowd in the strongest voice that he could muster. "This is so important to me, seeing my family together and seeing all my friends and neighbors. This is a Christmas that none of us will ever forget. Kammagar!"

Chapter 25

A GLORIOUS CHRISTMAS DAY

Andrew ran off with Sweetie and the neighborhood children looking for his presents. He was disappointed when he didn't find a knife like the one carried by Grandpa, but he was a sensible child, and figured Santa was extremely busy this time of year and maybe next year the knife would come. But he did find books and toys, and DVD movies, and the children sat around in a circle discussing what they had received and how they would share the bounty.

Out of sight of John, the neighborhood ladies had prepared a Christmas morning feast that would rival the most exclusive buffet in a five-star hotel. The food was fresh and healthy. John spotted his cinnamon rolls and when he started for the table, Anna gave him a plate of food that had many of his favorites, including the cinnamon rolls still steaming from the oven. Doc had the coffee ready, a pot of hearty Starbuck Kenya that he carried with him from Oregon.

As promised at the International Airport, the Customs man from Asor showed up with his wife and children and a huge plate of sashimi and sushi. John recognized him right away as one of his former top students. They shook hands and his wife fixed John a healthy plate of fish and seaweed.

After breakfast, the adults, including Charley and Matsuo, exchanged gifts. There wasn't much that you could give a man that wore a thu, or a lady wearing only a lava-lava. Commercial gifts from the mall, held little value, or even interest, out on an island where the basics revolved around living simply and having food and shelter. Love was a given between committed lovers. So many of the gifts were from the heart and originally designed, like a specially crafted shell necklace, or a shark's tooth pendant hanging on a thin rope made from the stringy contents of a coconut. Several of the family had written poems and songs carefully printed on parchment paper like the finest calligraphy. Several of the children actually sang duets and put on skits. No finest, heartfelt gift could be found anywhere in the world.

Andre and Constantine had brought Army T-shirts for everyone, a very popular choice. T-shirts are always in demand, not only with the special, colorful designs representing something important to the islands, but it's tough to believe, that even dark-colored islanders can get sun-burned. The children particularly needed to wear shirts and also shade hats, when they swam and snorkeled for many hours.

Still working hard to get back into the family, Eduardo had brought boxes and boxes of chocolates from the Guam Troop Store for the ladies. He knew how to please the disstaffers and it worked. He found himself receiving hugs from his relatives and the neighbor ladies, and most importantly, giant hugs from Florencia. She even shyly gave him a quick kiss on the lips in full public view. He thought to himself, "If I can get high on a kiss from Florencia, why would I ever need narcotics again?"

Anna and Erica walked out a few minutes later, holding two birthday cakes with candles. It was Constantine and Andre's birthdays and everyone joined in and sang "Happy Birthday, and Many More." Anna said, "It seemed only fitting that it is Jesus' birthday and that we include the boys in the festivities."

Eduardo yelled out, "And we needed dessert, something sweet, after that wonderful morning feast." He raised his glass of juice and said, "Here's to Constantine and Andre, my brother and my nephew. Best wishes!" He earned a lot of smiles and another hug and kiss from Florencia.

CHRISTMAS IN THE TROPICS

Matsuo stood up, tapped his glass for attention, and declared, "I can never repay this beautiful reception and Christian friendship, but what I can do is relate a story as repayment. Want to hear a story of courage, friendship and determination and will attest to the strength of the human being?" Anyone visiting Micronesia can attest that story telling is a great tradition of the Micronesian islands. Some stories are legends – some are true – and some are in between and allows the listener to evaluate and how to fit it into their everyday lives. Most have a valuable moral.

Several of the adults replied, "Bring it on. We want to hear your story." The children joined the group, were quiet and attentive and sat behind the elders.

He began the story with an introduction, "This could be a true story – it doesn't matter if it's true or not. It's about two brave boys and has a meaning for all of us:"

"In World War II, the Americans ferociously struck at Truk Lagoon and sunk over sixty Japanese ships and destroyed more than 270 airplanes. It has been called the "Japanese Pearl Harbor." The sunken ships are known as the 'Ghost Fleet,' over 180,000 tons of Japanese ships were destroyed and now lay on the bottom of the lagoon, mostly near Tonoas and Fefan Islands. At the time as the American military drew closer, many of the Japanese civilians had been evacuated back to their home. However, when the evacuation order came, a 15-year-old Japanese boy named Nikko Kurassa was off in the mountains hiking with his Chuukese friend, Sabby Redilphy, and he missed his escape ship to Japan.

"Nikko saw the American dive bombers from the mountain top and observed hundreds of explosions and some of the ships sinking in the lagoon. He instantly knew that there would be no more evacuation ships and he was probably isolated on Chuuk and might be taken prisoner, or as the military had told everyone, he would be slowly tortured and then killed by the 'fiendish' Americans. Nikko and Sabby stayed hidden in the bushes so the low-flying, zooming American pilots couldn't see them.

"Sabby told him not to worry, that he could hide in the mountains. Sabnat promised to bring him food everyday. Brandishing their three-foot machetes, the boys built a lean-to hut for shelter in less than a day. There was plenty of water in a mountain spring for drinking and bathing."

Andrew raised his hand and then asked, "What happened to his mother and father?"

"The father was in the military and survived the attack from the Americans. But unfortunately, his mother was on one of the evacuation ships and she died in the battle when her ship sunk."

Paying close attention, Sweetie stated, "It was a good thing that Nikko missed the ship. Did he ever see his father again?"

"He never saw his father again on Chuuk. The father later escaped on a Japanese submarine and got to Tokyo safely. But Nikko didn't know this and he was getting real worried that he would be caught. He thought maybe someone would follow Sabby and then he would get turned in to the Americans.

"So Nikki decided to try and escape but he couldn't figure out where. He had no choice about trying to survive. He was in the middle of the Pacific Ocean. He talked to Sabby about his situation and together, they worked out a plan to sail to Satawal which is the eastern most island of Yap State. It would mean crossing hundreds of kilometers of open ocean. But Sabby was not worried – he said he knew where he could steal a Japanese canoe and they could slip out through the opening in the coral reef and head westward to Satawal. Sabby said that he had been to Satawal once, that he had a distant uncle there, and the natives spoke Chuukese and weren't afraid of the Japanese and would hide and help his friend. Nikko spoke basic Chuukese and Sabby was improving with his Japanese expressions, and between the two of them, they were able to communicate in their combination of languages. Sabby told him not to worry, that he would be able to talk to people on Satawal without much difficulty.

"Two nights later, they slipped out through Piaanu Pass in their stolen canoe with food and water lashed to the outrigger. Sabby had sailed around the Truk lagoon before but had never been on the open ocean. The huge rolling waves surprised and frightened them. The boys had a rudimentary hand-held compass that would take them through the Western Islands to Satawal, about three hundred miles. On the third day after a large freak wave hit them, Sabby accidentally dropped the compass overboard and at first they were alarmed; but they noticed they had been generally going westward, so they set their course on the basis of the sun. Also they figured they would sight land as they wove through the other island groups.

"A week went by, and the boys hadn't seen anything. Their little sail tore in a few places, and their water was running short. They rigged up a catchment system to capture the rain water, and Nikki had good luck in snagging fish with his trolling line. After the first storm and being tossed around on the waves, they had mixed feelings about going to Satawal. They had barely survived but now at least they had plenty of water.

Nikko laughed and said, "Are we sure we know what we're doing?"

Sabby replied, "Sure, no problem. We'll get to Satawal in a coupla months. I think we're going to get real tired of fish and rain water. How about some candy?"

"Now I know I'm hallucinating. I can almost taste that candy."

"Want me to describe some different flavors and textures?"

"You stop it right now. I'm salivating and losing too much water."

"What we do know is that we can't go back. Our Gods will protect us. Too much time involved to turn around; we'd never make it, and also the winds wouldn't cooperate. Sometimes we have doldrums and an hour later, we've got a squall condition."

Nikki looked northwest and saw what he perceived as palm trees. He couldn't believe that they might have found an island. To clear his vision, he shook his head and rubbed his eyes.

But suddenly Sabby cried out, "Land ahoy. I see a small atoll. It's barely above the water. My father told me one time that there was an atoll that you could only see at low tide. I think it was called Condor

Bank. He showed me on the map a long time ago and it's close to Satawal.

"That's means we're close?"

"Yeah, maybe about two more days of sailing. Should we go ashore at Condor?"

"Sure thing. It will be good to feel solid ground again and maybe there's something to eat there, other than fish."

"As the boys slid up their canoe onto the sandy beach, they noted the atoll looked deserted with no sign of life. There were no fires or trash.

"The boys found several straggly coconut trees and some kind of mongrel citrus, and both varieties were bearing fruit. They hacked open a coconut, and dove voraciously into the milk and coconut meat, and were soon smiling contentedly with a full-belly.

Nikko said, "I hope our stomachs can handle all this food, something different. I feel okay. How about you?"

"Yup, going down fine. I can almost feel new energy coming through the system. Let's try some of the citrus. My mother told me that if you don't get Vitamin C, you can catch scurvy. That's all we need out here. It makes your teeth fall out."

Nikko laughed and said, "Yuck. Let's get some citrus real fast." He guffawed and added, "Let's go to the other side of the islet and see if there's a fast-food restaurant. I would sure like some salty French fries."

'The boys stayed overnight and hoisted sail at daybreak. They were now nourished and feeling pretty good that they would see Satawal in a few days, that's if they didn't miss it by just a few kilometers."

Andrew raised his hand and asked, 'Weren't the boys getting scared that they were lost. I looked at the globe in school one day, and there's not much land out there. I'd be really frightened."

Matsuo answered, "I know the boys were scared. We would all be. They could just give up and fall in the water and drown. But these boys were brave and continued on. I think the new food gave them a lot more energy and some hope. They were also optimistic about the future. They weren't ready to quit."

CHRISTMAS IN THE TROPICS

Andrew stated, "I really like those boys. They were strong and courageous."

"Yes, they were and because they fearlessly sailed on for three more days, they came across another island called Pikelot. The people there received them with a big feast and drink. They were saved and so happy to be safe. They natives didn't care that Nikko was Japanese. A man from Pikelot had gone ahead to Satawal to tell the people about the boys.

"The boys rested for three days and then were guided down to Satawal where Sabby found his uncle. The uncle's family prepared a *mitmit,* a traditional feast with singing and dancing. Fortunately, the Big War had passed them by and as the boys grew into young men, they married on the islands and raised families. They became expert sailors and their skills were passed onto their sons."

"I gave you a lot of clues about Nikko. Can anybody imagine who I might be related to?"

John, Charley and Constantine already knew Matsuo's history but didn't say a word. Sweetie asked, "Can you give us another clue?"

"I am Pwo, a master navigator and have crossed the sea many times in a Micronesian outrigger canoe. I am not afraid of the sea."

Andrew raised his arm real high and said, "I know. I know! Nikko was your father."

"Very close. Nikko was my grandfather, and he taught me all about the sea, boating and navigation. Because of him, my father and I have both been designated as master navigators, not only by ocean organizations and also by tradition with our local peoples."

Andrew asked, "So how did Nikko see his father again?"

"Remember when I said he saw his father again in Tokyo? He went there with a college class from Yap Proper, and just for fun, he looked his father up in the phone book, and he found him. His father was still healthy and strong and had remarried and had another son and a daughter. He was surprised that Nikko was still alive. He thought he had disappeared at sea. They had a wonderful reunion but Nikko wanted to go back to Satawal."

Sweetie asked, "What happened to Sabby, your grandfather's best friend?"

"Glad you asked. Do you know the department store downtown, and the fishing and guide service. He became a prominent business-man and he started and owned those companies before he died. His children carry on and do many good things for the islands. They work on saving the environment and help support the church. All of Nikko and Sabby's children were successful and were brought up with a healthy respect for life and for the environment, and of course, divine intervention. They both felt that at anytime they could have died, but the Gods saved them, the Christian God for Sabby and the Shinto Divinity for Nikko."

Andrew stated, "I think it's a true story because you're here with us for Christmas."

"And it's a good story to hear at Christmas, about God saving the world and helping us all to be brave and strong."

John asserted, "It's a wonderful story, Matsuo. Thank you for shar-ing it with us, and for bringing the flotilla to Ulithi."

"Anything for you, my Friend. Merry Christmas!"

Chapter 26

GONE FISHING

Everything calmed down after Christmas Day and the human vibrations on the island took a break before probably ramping up again for New Year's Day. Most of the islanders decided to go home and await the New Year on home ground, and maybe have their own quiet celebrations after the party on Ulithi. Most Yapese like everything quiet and they often find loud sounds startling and alarming. In the last few days, they had more than their share of breaking their routines of easy and relaxed.

John had been feeling poorly and weaker, and he knew he was starting to fade after realizing that his plans of re-uniting the family had worked. The excitement and adrenaline that had kept him fired up was dissipating and he could feel a coldness, even a sorrow, building in his bones and muscles, and especially his heart rhythms. He was constantly pandiculating. Smiling, he thought back to what his mother always told him when he was feeling ill and weary, "Johnny, drink some papaya juice. You'll feel fine tomorrow." And he often did. Some of his friends in the Marianas used noni juice. He often thought he should have tried that when his heart condition first started.

Judging by his worsening irregular heart beat, he knew that his health problems would only intensify and he would find himself in a wheelchair before long. Or even in a coma like an unfeeling,

JOE RACE

unknowing lump of flesh; and then his family would have to make a decision of taking him off of machines. The docs called it "chronic heart failure and atrial fibrillation." He knew that he had to make his move. He learned the term neurasthenia to also explain his chronic fatigue and persistent aches. Drugs didn't seem to help; a tolerance or even a total disregard of his body was developing. He knew his body wasn't getting enough oxygen to keep it moving at a normal rate and depression was taking over his mind. The equation was basic – no fuel or energy for the body. Every moment was becoming erratic and unpredictable.

He knew a major storm was building from the east. He could see the obvious signs of foul weather on the horizon and feel the softness of the air changing. Constantine and Ronnie put up the typhoon shutters. That evening he observed where the canoes were tied and where the anchors were left laying on the shore. He watched where the ropes were and how they were tied, and what would be the faster direction for the canoe to break clear of the beach. He saw the wind was stronger from the east, the clouds getting darker, and that the currents would drive an unanchored boat out thorough the break in the reef. In the privacy of his bedroom, he wrote several notes and put them in an inconspicuous place where they wouldn't be found right away but would only be discovered after some searching for information about his disappearance.

And he knew exactly what he was going to do. He had been planning off and on for several days. He slid into bed but didn't take any pain or sleeping medication. He waited until Anna came into the bedroom. He had prepared her medication for her high blood pressure, but had substituted a minor-dose sleeping tablet in place of her regular medication. Smiling, she took it and fell asleep almost immediately. He kissed her lightly on the forehead and her right cheek, and whispered, "Happy New Year. I love you." He could hear the storm building and felt the concrete walls shudder as the wind hit directly, probably 85 miles-per-hour gusts. He looked outside through the hurricane shutters and saw Constantine double-tying the canoes. They were bobbing up and down in the whitecaps.

CHRISTMAS IN THE TROPICS

John waited until Constantine went back into the house and saw no one else on the beach. He grabbed his long survival knife and walked out into the storm. The rain was almost horizontal driven by winds that had gone with tropical storm to near-typhoon conditions. Thunder boomed and lightning flashed, making the canoes visible sporadically. He was able to find his way just by feeling his all-familiar beach with his bare feet. He knew the storm was on him full-blast – the rain was dense against his face and the wind was heavier, almost knocking him over. But he hunched down, got to the water, found two anchors, cut them loose and dumped them in the canoe. He fell in the water as the waves were lapping at his ankles; but he managed to crawl to where the canoes were tied. He slashed the rope on the larger canoe and was able to roll inside the hull before it started to move at record speed with the easterly current. He dropped all the fishing tackle and sinkers that were still in the boat off the side in shallow water.

He threw his knife up onto the shore, knowing that his grandson Andrew had long admired the knife, an exact replica of a Jim Bowie design. He thought it strange that in the midst of this drama and trauma with rain and wind smashing on his face, he remembered the first knife his father had given him. It was a pen knife that he still used to sharpen his pencils and for whittling of birds and fish.

Within an hour, John knew he was beyond the reef and in open ocean territory. The depth of the ocean was probably over two thousand meters. He knew the approximate depth because he had often fished in this area, but truthfully had never found bottom. The wind and rain continued to blast him. He knew his strength was fading and he felt a heart attack or stroke would be coming on soon. He deftly tied one of the anchors to the canoe, so it would ride slow in the current and not go too far out into the open ocean, knowing the islanders would need the canoe for subsistence fishing. It was one of his all-time favorite boats. He tied the second rope and anchor around his ankles. For the last few moments of his life, he was part of a cascading, churning mayhem. He was lifted high on the crests, than dropped hard into a trough. He let the tempest do its job and within minutes the canoe flipped over while cresting a monstrous twelve-foot wave, and threw him into the whirling water. It was done – there was no turning back.

John was temporarily startled by the surging waters when he splashed down, and he began to struggle for survival, a natural response to his drowning. The suffocation and fighting for air was painful and terrifying. Then he remembered this was part of his plan to return to nature and be part of it forever. He willed himself to stop struggling and the anchor pulled him deeper and deeper. He thought of Anna, now like a surreal dream, like life in another plane, another dimension of the universe. He sucked some water into his lungs. His last thoughts were about how smooth the water felt, how he sluiced through it at super speed, and how it began to get colder as he went deeper. Then the complete darkness of the depths turned off his mind and he was gone. He was home.

Next morning the family noticed that John and Anna didn't leave their room for breakfast. This was unusual because the two were usually the first ones up, getting the coffee and eggs ready. Constantine knocked on their door but there was no answer. He opened the unlocked door, and Anna was still sleeping but his Papa was gone. After some effort, he woke up Anna, and she was in a groggy, dizzy state and had no idea where Papa was.

Constantine rounded up the family and asked them to start looking for Papa. The storm had subsided and even the sun was trying to break through the remaining clouds. No one had seen Papa. Eduardo came running in and said, "There's a canoe missing. Maybe the storm took it but the rope looks like it's been cut with a sharp knife."

"How about the anchors?"

"Two missing and the two lines cut also. Papa's survival knife and some fishing equipment were in shallow water near the cut lines." Eduardo gave the knife to Andrew to hold for safekeeping until Papa came back in.

"Ronnie, how about you and Eduardo take the motorboat and do a check around the lagoon. Maybe Papa ended up stranded in one of the coves. Helen, you and Erica start calling all the neighbors. Belle and I will try and get hold of the rescue boat in Colonia. Hopefully all the telephone lines and satellites are working so we can get through to anyone."

By the end of the day, no one had any success in finding Papa. Anna still felt drowsy and very worried, saying that she hadn't felt this way since she and Papa had got drunk one time in college to find out how it felt. She said that was the last time they tried it. She said that she felt stupid for two days.

Anna said that she needed to shower and try and wake up. As she was adjusting the lotions on her dresser, she came across several notes, one was a very personal love letter to her. It was a heartfelt, beautiful note from John. It said:

My dearest love:

I have always loved you since I the first time I saw you on the beach. This has been a very meaningful, beautiful Christmas, and I will always be watching over you. I hope it helped to bring our family back together.

Please forgive me for what I am about to do – but it is for the best. I do not want to be an invalid or a burden to you and the family. I know my health is fading fast at an accelerated rate. I can feel it inside. After my life of freedom on the open seas, I cannot imagine how terrible it would be to be tied to a machine to help me breathe and to keep my heart going in some sterile hospital.

This is for the best. I am going fishing and won't be back. My physical body will be part of the ocean but my spirit will be in Heaven. I will be waiting for you.

You are a wonderful, loving person. I will be thinking of you always and watching down on you and the family from above. Thank you for a wonderful Christmas. God bless you!

Love forever, John, your Lover Boy

She put it in a safe place in her purse. The other two were general in nature. She didn't tell anyone right away but she now knew now what had happened.

She began crying and sobbed all night. It was her private grieving time. The children didn't see her for eight hours – they didn't worry about her and figured she was just sleeping because of the stress and tension.

The following day, a massive Taiwanese fishing boat came across an overturned canoe outside the Ulithi channel. It was dragging an anchor and the word "Ulithi" was painted on its hull. There was no sign of a survivor. The fishing ship was bound for Yap Proper to renew its fishing license. Two local fishermen passed by in another canoe and saw the Ulithi canoe, and told the Chinese captain they knew who owned it and where it belonged. The captain slowed his ship and released the canoe and the fishermen managed to upturn the canoe and pull in the anchor. They took it in tow and sailed to Falealop Island. The fishermen had heard that John was missing, and unfortunately, they knew they would be the bearers of sad news.

As the fishermen slid their canoe onto the Sapelalut beach and they yelled out, the family came pouring out from everywhere on the property. The family members had had no luck in finding John, nor had the rescue boat and the Coast Guard helicopter. When Constantine saw the empty canoe, his worst thoughts were realized, and he and the other family member knew that Papa was gone, probably drowned during the wild storm. He never wore a safety life jacket.

Eduardo thanked the fishermen and gave them dinner. The fishermen left off three large mahi-mahi fish and they were soon on their way to their island, so their families wouldn't be worrying.

About an hour later, Anna took the two oldest children, Constantine and Helen into her bedroom. She showed them the notes. She didn't mention her very personal, love letter which she had secreted away.

Anna said, "Papa never drowned accidentally. You know that he had enough sense not to go out in a tropical storm? He knew the ocean well."

Constantine said, "We thought that also but we had to go through the motions."

"We all knew what Papa wanted," added Helen.

Anna asserted, "Papa has considered everything with those notes. He knew he had to cover the family's insurance programs, his retirement pension, and reputation, and be okay with the church."

Helen asked, "How much should we let the family know?"

Constantine stated, "Let's just follow what Papa wanted. We'll just do what the notes say to do. No sense in starting gossip and getting everybody arguing."

"Okay with me. Here's a match," said Helen. She lit the one note and the attachments on fire, and the ashes fell into an empty bowl. She concluded, "I'll save the note Papa said to give to the police. It'll be safe with me."

Anna wrinkled her brow and said, "Papa went fishing, and just had a bad accident. That's it. What a brave man to go out in that storm!"

"Bad things happen to good people, even at Christmas-time." Constantine gathered both ladies under his arms and they hugged tightly.

EPILOGUE

John Sapelalut had led a full, meaningful life, and had made many significant contributions to the State of Yap and to the world in general. He had raised four wonderful children and his blood ran in the veins of the grandchildren, who were showing great promise in the fields of sport, government and education. He was always a good citizen, and dabbled in politics occasionally, helping to write the new Yapese Constitution when it was decided to join the Federated State of Micronesia, and be part of a new emerging country. He was a nice man, a very kind man, an excellent teacher.

On the day after Christmas, Anna, Helen and Constantine had discussed the two notes, the first was simply addressed to Anna and said, "Gone fishing for a few hours. Will be back soon. Love, Johnny Boy." John had paper clipped a small note that said, "Note for the insurance company and the police – destroy this attachment after reading the note. Give the note to the authorities." The second note simply said, "To all family members – Thank you for being such good people and supporting me in everything I tried to do. Gone to the other side. Will be watching over you. Love and hugs always from Papa." The note attached to this message was "Destroy all of this. Do not share with anyone."

The parish priest thought his disappearance at sea was unusual, and maybe even looked like a suicide. Therefore if that was the case, a mass would not permitted by the canons of the church; but the priest decided to have a service in his honor anyway, and wrote his disappearance off as a misfortune during fishing on the open seas. A week afterwards the family had an island-wide celebration, inviting friends and family, and included the politicians and leaders from Yap Proper.

The church-goers were accustomed to solemn, serious funerals and memorial services, and weren't quite prepared for a celebration with music and dancing. They had watched some of the noisy funeral processions from New Orleans on television, and never did quite grasp all the commotion and loud brass instruments. But John had written in his will that he would like a nice send-off to Heaven with lots of music and joyfulness, and money saved on the funeral could be used for a feast and to rent a launch to bring over visitors, not only from Yap proper but also from the outer islands. He wanted several old classmates to fly in from Palau.

Anna was exhausted after not sleeping properly while the search for John was going on and preparing for the memorial service. She knew that he had chosen to take the way out that fit into his personal code – he was tired of lying around feeling useless and was really worried about being an invalid and a burden to everyone in the family. They had talked about this on several of his most depressing days. She always tried to cheer him up but she could see in his eyes that he was deciding and making plans of his own. She knew him only too well. He would pat her arm and say, "Just relax, my Darling Woman. Enjoy your Christmas with the family." She let these moments pass, trying to believe that John wouldn't do anything foolish and leave them too soon.

So Anna let her two sons and two daughters do the planning and organizing for the church service, and they did it superbly. The mass had gone well, and she felt John's spirit was in the church sitting next to her. The priest delivered a powerful sermon about the sanctity of human existence and talked about John's life. The children had selected Constantine to deliver a eulogy about their father, and he did it well, covering the main parts of his life and including the feelings and sentiments contributed by Anna. There was a great hush in the church when the children sang two of John's favorite hymns. Tears flowed freely, men and women alike.

The feast and celebration would never be forgotten on Ulithi. All the important dignitaries were there, along with John's personal friends, and hundreds of the extended family. He wasn't a celebrity or a high profile politician, but he was a decent man who had impacted many, many lives. The celebration lasted for two days, and because of a few rain clouds, the family put up overhead tarps, and the visitors snuggled under the coverings or found a dry place in the main house, in the added family rooms or in Doc's thatched hut. No one was left out in the rain or went without food and drink. John's disappearance and probable death had united old friends and family into a new relationship and made them all stronger in appreciating life and then facing their own demise.

John had brought the family together for Christmas and their lives had been touched by his loving hands and had taken on new, promising dimensions and directions. There was a new enjoyment for life everyday. Minor irritations no longer mattered. Material goods like gold and diamonds were just words in the dictionary.

John's body was never found, but his spirit was with them always.

After the feast, friends and dignitaries drifted off to their normal routines. Seeing the magic and blessings of the Christmas season, their lives were memorably touched forever. Doc and his family left right after New Year's Day and thanked everyone in the family for letting them be part of such a personal experience. The daughters had earned their scuba license and had taken magnificent photographs. Hillary wanted to come again next school break and bring along one of her classmates for the rewarding experience. Doc asked Anna, after hugging, "Are you going to be okay. Do you need anything?"

She replied, "No, I'm fine. We both know what a good man he was."

"And a very spiritual, strong man. None of us will ever forget him."

Anna had a few lugubrious weeks but gradually she grew more vigorous, avoiding depression, and was able to successfully function. She watched for John in every sunset. She kept her handicraft business moving right along not losing a beat, did some travel, and eventually she joined the senior citizens' group and learned to play canasta and bingo. She went to Guam and helped Belle fix up her new apartment. She had a lot of laughs and good food, and met several interesting "gentlemen." Her main interests remained her children and the grandchildren, especially the new ones that kept coming. John's legacy continued on.

Anna erected a small granite memorial near the canoes so that ever time the family went to the boats or swimming, there would be a permanent marker about Grandpa John, and how he had affected so many lives positively and forever. Along with his name, these words were simply engraved: "Papa went fishing – will be back soon!"

Andre and Vicky returned to the military at leave's end and completed their discharges. On their return to their military assignments, they learned that the First Sergeant had been re-assigned to Iraq and had driven over an IED on his second day in country. His driver had been killed, and he had lost most of his right leg below the thigh. After the discharges, the lovers moved temporarily to Tennessee with her parents, and had an old-fashioned traditional wedding in March, complete with tuxes and big fluffy dresses. Of all their congratulory notes, the most memorable one was from the First Sergeant; he said, "Glad you got out Vicky. You would have rotated to Iraq if you had stayed. Don't worry about me – I had already given up playing soccer. Love and best wishes to you both, Sarge." The lovers planned on honeymooning in Japan and Yap, and then starting their college classes in Nashville, Tennessee. Country music was not new to Andre. Most of the guys in his unit could hum the new songs and knew all about Tim McGraw, Alabama, Taylor Swift, Carrie Underwood, Garth Brooks, and Brooks and Dunn. Vicky soon had him dressing up in cowboy togs with a big black hat and pointy-toed leather boots. He liked to say, "Now I can hammer those cockroaches hiding in the corners."

Constantine decided not to re-enlist and by the time he got back to Guam, Belle had fixed up a beautiful apartment with a never-ending view of the Philippines Sea and a separate bedroom for Sweetie. Belle had finished her classes and had passed her exams for marriage and family counselor, got licensed and had landed a job with the Guam Health Services. She told Constantine that after he relaxed and decompressed after Iraq and his many years of military service, she had made a contact at the airlines for him to interview for a mechanic's job. She told him that if he liked it, there would be flight privileges that would allow them to travel all over the world. He jokingly replied, "As long as it isn't the Middle East." He told her that he had a special surprise for her when he landed on Guam and to bring Leilani along.

At the airport a few days later, Belle spotted him right away, and behind him was Jeremy "Jerry" Simpson, a longtime ex-Army friend, and recently divorced. Leilani already knew him and in the past, had found him attractive with an endless sense of humor. He kept her happy and smiling. At the time, she wished he had been single. Belle asked her, "Do you suppose that's the surprise?"

"Sister, I hope so. He is one handsome man. *Machismo*."

"Yep, but I thought you believed all men were dogs. Not worth your time. Too much hassle."

"Maybe an exception is in order. He's looking at me and smiling. I'm getting weak-kneed like a school girl." She paused and said, "Holy carambra, he's throwing me a kiss." Her face flushed.

"Have fun but don't stay out too late, Sister. You talk to him, and I'm going to grab my big strong civilian. He's going to be in my bed every night. No more cots and tents for my man."

Ronnie and Helen continued on, bonded tighter with new strengths from the family and a stronger sense of being part of the overall scheme of life. Their marriage remained committed and their love everlasting. Helen asked Ronnie, "Do you think our love could be as strong as the love that my Mother and Father shared?" He simply raised his eyebrows island-style, meaning "Of course." No further words were necessary. They went back to Oregon and Ronnie continued to write and she did the editing as well as watching over their toddler, and of course in a few months, delivered a new baby with John's blood. One Sapelalut passed on, and a new one came aboard. They called their new son John Junior.

Eduardo was a changed man. It was like his interior lights finally went on inside the noggin and he decided to grow up and realize what was important in leading a constructive life. Words and drugs like blow, acid, quaaludes, xanax, meth, grass and opiates were no longer in his vocabulary. He was now into the best design and effectiveness of fishing lures, or the faster growing seeds on the little farm that he started behind Anna's house. Florencia played a major role in his new life. He had foregone the drugs and booze on his own and escaped his juvenile, loser label, but now this island woman was turning him into a man of caring and sensitivity, and something he had never experienced, sweat and hard work. He loved to watch his seeds germinate in the rich soil, and felt proud to bring home fish for the family after a successful day on the sea. It took some doing, but his brothers and neighbors taught him to bring in the big ones. Andrew followed him everywhere, like his friendly shadow. He enjoyed being with her children and they soon started calling him Papa Ed.

Every time the children interacted with him, Florencia would smile and clap her hands, like he had won a great championship. But it was significantly more important than any contest or lottery — Eduardo had won the love and respect of a ready-made family, who were returning his love. He was over-whelmed every day for how his life was changing, and all because of Papa wanting the family back together for the holidays. He loved the way Florencia wore her ebony black hair in braids with colorful bows, the ends dropping past her backside.

Erica received a letter inside of a larger envelope that had been mailed to Anna Sapelalut. A young man from Maap, Joey Yinez was expressing his sorrow and sending condolences for the loss of a man most influential in his life – Mr. Sapelalut had been his teacher for two years at Yap High School.

Erica carefully opened the enclosed letter from Joey. The epistle was short and to the point, and as she read it slowly, tears began to swell from her eyes. His handwriting was precise and artistic, like all youngsters are taught in Yap. It read:

"I hope my letter finds you happy and well. I always think of you, and your big, glorious smile, and the good times that we had together. You said you would write and you didn't. I sent a dozen letters to my mother to forward to you in Ulithi and asked her to send any responses back to me. She said you weren't interested and only wanted to take care of your family.

I understand that and commend your commitment to your family. But if you can, please write me and tell what you are doing. Did you get married? Have you gone to college? I will graduate in a few months and will start my medical training in Portland, Oregon. I want to be a surgeon and maybe help out at home. Want to be my office nurse? (ha-ha).

If you ever get to the mainland, please look me up. I can show you so many new and exciting things. I have met some pleasant girls here, but none as nice and pretty like you. Please write. I would love to hear from you.

Your friend always, Joey

P.S. Here's some hugs for you – OOOOO – don't be offended ok?

Erica read and re-read the letter a dozen times. She was ebullient, breaking into tears of joy. Anna asked her why she was crying. She answered, "I've been thinking of Joey for over five years and now I find out he was thinking of me, and his mother was lying to both of us. She had no right to keep my letters from him. She wouldn't even give me his address so I could write direct."

Anna said, "Don't be too harsh on his mother. In her mind, she wanted what was best for him, to have a professional job and a good life with his university diploma. She got tied down on the island and it's not wrong for parents to want something better for their children. You know what happens to many of the young people here. They get married, then have children, and never realize their dreams. You now have a big chance in your life – don't let your hurt and angst overshadow this wonderful opportunity for your future. You still can still follow your heart with Joey, if you still like him."

"You're right but why wouldn't I still like him?"

"People change in five years, even island boys. Maybe he's a drunk, or egotistic or a selfish pinhead. There's only one thing to do. Go visit him after the New Year's celebration. You won't know until you see him. He left his address and phone number on the envelope."

"What would Papa think? Maybe I'm being too forward."

"Two things to remember. First, you know Papa – he was always ready for travel and an adventure. Second, if Joey works out and you both like each other, he would want you to be happy and find the right partner for your future. You have enough money saved for your ticket."

"Do you think I should call him?"

"No time like the present, Baby Girl. If you don't go college on Guam with Constantine and Belle, you can always go to college in Oregon; and two can almost live as cheaply as one. You need to get this matter taken care of while you can. You can't keep worrying and thinking about something that might never happen."

Nervously and almost shaking, Erica called. As luck would have it, he answered on the second ring. They talked and talked, and reminisced about their school days and swimming in the lagoon. Erica laughed out loud a dozen times and cried twice. Anna kept pointing at her watch, reminding her of the long distance charges from their remote island.

She said, "Okay, Mom. I understand. I'll hang up in just a few minutes." She laughed a few more times, and finally hung up with the biggest smile Anna had ever seen on her little girl.

"Well? What happened?" asked Anna.

"It's all good news. First of all, he's the same old Joey. He's still nice and sweet, and still has that delightful sense of humor. We're going to write each other long letters, do some e-mails and discuss our futures, mainly about long term ambitions and later about marriage and a family. He has my direct addresses now, and phone number, so no more mother interference."

"Is he angry with his mother? I hope not."

"He's kind of upset, but understands. Because of her love and concern, and pushing him all the time, he's going to graduate in premed. She's coming for his graduation in May. And you know what else? Are you ready for this?"

"What else?"

"He wants me to come a month earlier than graduation so we can get to know each other. His regular college roommate has dropped out, so there's plenty of room for me at his apartment. His college is so close I would only have to walk three blocks. Joey knows all the school counselors. It's all so wonderful!"

"It is so, and you can make things happen," said Anna, thinking of John and their college years together. She added, "Papa was right about getting us all together. This has been a wonderful Christmas. He's watching down on you this very moment and wishing you well."

Erica said, "I love my Papa."

"Me too, Baby Girl! Me too…" They hugged, and looked off to the horizon.

The sun was setting, the sky still a rich iridescent blue but fading into a kaleidoscope of red, orange and pink. The infinite shades of green in the jungle were turning darker, but still bright and shiny, almost glowing after a short rain shower. Christmas had left its magic on the island. A slight breeze rippled the placid waters on the lagoon. Two dolphins were jumping and playing, and singing their mysterious songs.

GLOSSARY:

(All words Yapese unless other wise noted)

Beche-de-mer- sea slugs, used for food, thought to be an aphrodisiac by the Chinese

Betir – daughter

Bula-bula – an exaggeration, boastful (Filipino)

Chicharrones – crispy pig skin, comes in a bag like potato chips (Chamorro)

Cruci figo – fasten to a cross, crucifixion (Latin)

Dapal – women's house

Faluw – men's house

Finadene – sauce/topping made from soy, vinegar, onion, local peppers (Saipan)

Galoof – monitor lizard

Garfoko – beloved one

Kammagar - thank you, showing appreciation

Kau – shells used as money

Kefel – goodbye, adios

Latte – large stone foundations upon which Chamorros built a home (Saipan)

Lava-lava – woman's skirt made of hibiscus and banana fiber, or cotton cloth

Lechon – cooked pig/pork – many different recipes in the islands

Lei – a necklace of flowers, e.g., plumerias, orchids (Ponapeian)

Lengin – wife

Machismo – masculine, strong male (Spanish)

Madangadang – member of the noble class

Maganda – pretty, beautiful (Filipino Tagalog)

Mahalo – thank you (Hawaiian), used all over the Pacific

Mitmit – a traditional feast with singing and dancing

Mogethin – hello, a greeting

Mwar-mwar – flowery headband, crown of flowers (Ponapeian)

Nanyochokan – Japanese headquarters on Koror, Palau

Nanyo Gunto – Japanese name for Micronesia

Pebai – men's meeting house

Pilune - chief

Pin - woman

Rai – ancient stone money – up to 13-feet across

Rau – red

Sirow - excuse me, pardon me

Tagil – village, place

Talayeru – traditional fishing practices (Chamorro)

Taro – starchy, elephant-eared tuber, a staple food for many Pacific islanders

Thu – men's loincloth, color reflecting island origin

Toming – Japanese low-class name for Micronesians

Tuba – an island alcoholic drink fermented from the coconut tree blossom

Ub – come!

Voi - Polynesian chestnut

Wa'ab – Yapese name for Yap Proper

Wunbey – a Yapese stone platform

Yar – necklaces of oyster shells